Copyright © 2024 by Dr Surinder Singh Jolly MBE

Published by Blazing Eyes Publishing

All rights reserved.

No part of this book may be reproduced in any form or by any electronic or mechanical means, including information storage and retrieval systems, without written permission from the author, except for the use of brief quotations in a book review.

This is a work of fiction. All names, characters, places, events, incidents, businesses and industries in this book are either the product of the author's imagination or used in a fictitious manner. Any resemblance to actual persons, living or dead, or actual events is purely coincidental.

TSUNAMI OF GREED

SURINDER SINGH JOLLY

ALSO BY SURINDER SINGH JOLLY

Indian Whispers

ACKNOWLEDGEMENTS

Thank you to my wife, Gursharan. Her invaluable support made this book possible.

Thanks to my daughters, Jasleen, Ishveen and Kavneet for all their encouragement. Any IT and other issues, I would telephone them and they were always kind and helpful to dad.

1

20th June 1996

It was Bobby Kohli's 80th birthday. His wife Pinky had spent the day decorating their Bradford home with balloons and banners.

A childless couple, their home was nevertheless filled with love and laughter. Both loved music and parties. A good singer, Bobby, and a lovely dancer, Pinky, were the centre of any party.

The doorbell rang. Bobby opened the door.

Standing outside was his nephew, Paul, holding a bouquet of red roses.

"Happy birthday, Uncle."

"What a pleasant surprise! Did you drive all the way from Edinburgh?"

"Especially for you."

"I wish my brother Ranjit had also come. You know, he is only two years younger than me."

"Yeah, dad would have liked to," replied Paul. "He sends his best wishes, though."

Inside, Paul helped to get the lounge ready for the party and soon others started arriving,

Bobby introduced Paul to his friends. It was a sunny summer day. Paul placed chairs in the garden and served the drinks to the guests.

When everyone had arrived, they gathered in the lounge where Bobby blew out candles and cut the big birthday cake, as his friends cheered his name.

Champagne flowed with the music and laughter.

Pinky, petite with long fair hair, wearing a golden silk sari with a gold bindi on her forehead, held Bobby's hands.

As they danced together, Bobby looked into Pinky's eyes and whispered, "Your flashing brown eyes and radiant smile remind me of our first date when you were sweet sixteen. I love you, my soulmate."

After the dance, Paul came over and hugged Bobby. "I wish you a long, healthy life with love forever."

Overflowing with whisky and dancing, the party finished late into the night.

In bed, Bobby was restless.

"What's wrong?" asked Pinky.

"Indigestion. Overeaten."

Pinky went to fetch the indigestion medicine and when she returned from the kitchen, Bobby was sitting on the bed profusely sweating with both his hands on his chest.

Hands shaking, Pinky called the emergency number. An ambulance arrived within five minutes.

The paramedics did an ECG recording of his heart and Bobby was taken away on a stretcher with an oxygen mask on.

Inside the ambulance, Pinky sat holding Bobby's hands. She felt her heart thumping fast.

She closed her eyes and prayed. *God, please save my Bobby.*

Paul drove behind the ambulance.

On arriving at the hospital, Bobby was rushed to the coronary care unit where he was placed in a bed attached to the cardiac monitor and oxygen. The doctors examined him and gave him an injection.

They reassured him.

Bobby smiled at Pinky, asking her to sit on his bed. Holding her hands, he whispered, "Don't worry. Be strong."

Then he turned to Paul. "Look after Pinky."

"I promise you, I will. I am your son. I love you both."

"We are blessed to have you, son ..."

Suddenly, Bobby looked pale, grey, sweaty. He collapsed on the bed.

Pinky screamed. "Help! Doctor, doctor!"

The doctor and nurses came running.

They closed the curtain around the bed. Pinky was crying.

Several agonising minutes later, the doctor opened the curtain slightly. Looking at his serious face, Pinky knew that the devastating news was coming. Her heart almost stopped.

"So sorry that we could not save Bobby despite our best efforts," whispered the doctor.

Paul helped Pinky to sit in a chair.

Wiping her tears, she asked, "Is this a nightmare?"

The nurse took them to the side room and gave them tea. "The doctor will join you soon."

PINKY REMEMBERED NOTHING OF THE DRIVE HOME.

Once there, she sat on her bed, confused. *It was his happy birthday, not a day to die. What happened?*

She repeated this again and again. She did not sleep all night.

In the morning, Paul brought her tea and toast. "Please look after yourself. Bobby told you to be strong. Don't worry, I'll help you."

"Without Bobby, my life is not worth living," Pinky replied.

2

The funeral director was contacted. Knowing Sikhs believe in cremation, he advised Paul to get a cremation certificate. *It is mandatory before any cremation.*

The funeral date was fixed for 28th June.

All of Bobby's friends and family were contacted. Pinky had already talked to Bobby's sister in India.

On the morning of the funeral, Bobby was washed and dressed in new clothes by his male relatives and friends.

Paul tied a tie on Bobby. It matched his new suit. Friends had tears in their eyes as they thought of Bobby when he was alive.

The crematorium was full, with people standing outside.

Tributes were paid to Bobby. One charity worker from Bradford city centre described how Bobby and his team would cook meals in the Gurdwara-Sikh temple. He would take them to city centre to feed the homeless people every weekend. If anyone thanked him, he would reply, "It is my duty. In my faith, helping people who are less fortunate is our duty to humanity."

Bobby's elder sister Jasmeet shed light on Bobby's life.

"Bobby was born 1916 in Amritsar, India. On 13th April 1919, when he was three years and I was five years old, we lost both our parents in the firing by soldiers of the then Indian British rulers. On that fateful day, Bobby and Ranjit (aged one year) stayed with grandfather, but I accompanied my parents.

"We were brought up by our grandfather. He taught us respect and service to humanity. On cold winter nights we used to accompany him as he covered poor people sleeping on pavements with warm blankets.

"Bobby studied engineering and decided to come to UK in 1960. Jobs were difficult to come by. He worked in a shoe factory. Then he successfully opened his own factory, making shoes which were exported all over the world. Behind my brother's success was Pinky, his wife and best friend."

The last speaker was a close friend. "A life well lived. A happy man, giving joy to others. Bobby lived a rich life. Rest in peace, my friend." Tears welled up in his eyes.

A Sikh priest read Kirtan Sohila, the last prayer before the cremation.

All then stood for the final prayers.

At the end of the service, the screen started closing.

As the coffin became obscured from view, Pinky sobbed uncontrollably. Supporting her were her friends and Jasmeet.

As the mourners were leaving the cremation hall, they lined up to express their condolences.

Seeing their love, Pinky's eyes filled with tears.

3

One night before leaving for India, Jasmeet hugged Pinky and told her, "I will pray in the Amritsar's Golden Temple for my brother's soul and your wellbeing."

She also gave her a book.

"What is it?" asked Pinky.

"After I retired as headmistress of a girls' school, I found the courage to write about my memories of the 1919 Amritsar massacre. The five-year-old girl in these pages is me. I gave her my name Jasmeet, as it is a true story."

Pinky began reading the very next day.

13th April 1919, Amritsar

Five year-old Jasmeet looked out of the window at the people dancing to Bhangra drums in the park opposite her house.

She ran into the kitchen. "Mum, papa, let's go to the park. People are dancing. Children have balloons in their hands. There are food stalls. We'll have fun."

Papa said, "Yes, we'll go to the park but first we'll visit the Gurdwara to say prayers. Today is the Sikh festival of Vaisakhi."

Jasmeet had never been so quick in the bath, and then her mother combed her long hair and made two lovely braids. Jasmeet put on a new Salwar Kameez, just like her mum.

Her dad wore a saffron orange turban.

Jasmeet asked her dad, "Why are we all wearing the same coloured clothes?"

"It is Kesari-saffron orange colour. It represents courage and wisdom. After all, today is our religious festival of Vaisakhi."

Jasmeet jumped around like a little goat. Mum smiled, noticing how excited Jasmeet was. They started walking and joined hundreds of worshippers going towards Harmandir Sahib, also called the Golden Temple. On entering the massive Gurdwara complex, they walked on the marble walkway around the huge pool. Mum looked at Jasmeet. She had covered her head with Kesari dupatta. She told her she looked so cute.

They reached the causeway over the pool. Jasmeet wanted to run but there were so many pilgrims. It took them an hour to reach the inner sanctum. Once inside, Jasmeet knelt and bowed on the floor in front of the holy book, Guru Granth Sahib. She then stood up, closed her eyes and said her prayers.

When they came out of the inner sanctum, Jasmeet tugged her dad. "Let's go to the park now."

"We can't go without eating langar."

"Why?"

"Don't you know? Since Guru Nanak more than four hundred years ago started free food for all the needy people, langar is part of our religion. You can eat a little here and the rest in the park."

Jasmeet reluctantly agreed. In the past, she had seen her mother making chapattis in the kitchen with other volunteers. There were hundreds of people in the massive halls where langar was served. They sat on the ground together just like the Sikh gurus commanded that all, irrespective of caste, rich or poor should sit together as equal and eat the same food. The volunteers served chapatis, rice, daal-lentils, vegetable curry and kheer, a dessert.

At last, they started walking to the park, a short distance away. They could hear children whooping and playing, vendors selling their wares, people chanting slogans, a whole array of different singers and styles, while the dhol drums drowned them out. The air felt alive with people who had travelled from hundreds of miles around to be in Amritsar for Vaisakhi.

At the entrance of the park, soldiers were trying to push an armoured car through a narrow passage.

"Dad, why are they carrying guns?"

Dad replied, "They are protecting the Indian British rulers."

He then said, laughing, "They'll never be able to get their car through the entrance. Can't they see how narrow it is?"

Dark clouds appeared in the sky. Thousands of people were crammed into the small park surrounded by arched walls with a well in the centre. Men were wearing saffron orange turbans and women were dressed in every colour and pattern you could think of. Jasmeet couldn't remember seeing so many people in one place before and the buzz filled her with joy and excitement.

Papa said, "Every year on Vaisakhi day, villagers from the surrounding countryside visit the Gurdwara and then they come to this park, the Jallianwala Bagh, to have fun and reflect. Vaisakhi was a time where our tenth guru, Guru Gobind Singh Ji, brought together the values of Sikhism and made sure every Sikh knew their duty to promote equality and freedom; and to stand up against injustice wherever we see it."

In the corner of the park a small group of people listened to a speaker, who was standing on a bench. They started shouting, "Inquilab Zindabad – long live the revolution."

"Papa, why are they shouting?"

"They are protesting against the British rule in India. I heard that some Indian leaders have been arrested."

Jasmeet ran towards a vendor with brightly coloured balloons in his hands, the kind she loved to play with and carry around. She jumped as she suddenly heard several loud bangs in a row and as she looked up, she saw the balloons flying away. The noises around her had changed, no longer the sound of laugher but still loud and reverberating around the park. She turned to the vendor, on her lips a question about the balloons, but she froze. He had slumped to the ground. There was a pool of blood where he fell. Jasmeet looked back at her parents and saw her mother on the ground too. She was confused. She ran to her mother. The loud noises had turned to screams and panic whilst the loud bangs continued relentlessly. Her mother lay motionless. As Jasmeet clung to her, her hands became sticky and her clothes turned red with her mother's blood. She understood only when she looked around and saw the panic as people were running and being shot at by soldiers who had surrounded the park. Her throat felt dry. She could feel the terror inside her and the tears running down her cheeks.

She felt herself being picked up away from her mum, and found her Papa's arms tight around her as he sprinted.

She saw a child being trampled under the feet of rushing crowds and gripped her father's neck even tighter. As she watched the crowds and people falling down around her with horror, she felt her dad stumble and fall on top of her in the well. She screamed from the ground as she looked at his face contorted with pain, eyes half closed and arms slackening around her. She continued to cling, even as the gunshots continued, even as she felt her Papa's body become heavy on top of her, even as she felt pools of blood from him. She closed her eyes and gripped her Papa tightly.

She did not know how long it took until she opened her eyes again. Before anything, the putrid smell hit her. She stayed cowering under her father's body, now cold and stiff as she looked out and saw people being dragged out of the well, bodies on stretchers and the ground stained with blood. Disorientated and scared, she couldn't fully comprehend what had happened. She felt herself being dragged away from her father and screamed, not wanting to leave him. Arms held her, voices around her spoke softly and she could feel herself being carried away as her eyes closed and she lost consciousness.

Forty-five years later with her granddaughter, she returned to the site of the massacre, Jallianwalla Bagh. All the painful memories of that day flooded back. How would she explain that day to her five-year-old granddaughter now?

She too had been five years old on that fateful day in 1919. Afterwards, her childhood had been lonely and full of fear. While other children played outdoors, she stayed in her house. Every Diwali, when children and their parents celebrated with fireworks, she hid in her room. Every firecracker sound brought flashbacks of shootings and bleeding bodies. She would feel the blood of her parents in her hands and her shirt felt wet and warm. She would climb into her bed with a photograph of her parents and pray and pray until she fell asleep. The trauma stayed with her all her life.

With the passage of time, India had gained independence from the British in 1947 and Jasmeet had learned the true horror of what had happened that day and how it had contributed towards the downfall of the Empire. How this massacre had led to protests all over India and how people had embodied the spirit of Vaisakhi by standing up to the British rule, even if it cost them their lives.

Today, on her fiftieth birthday, she had plucked up the courage to return to the Jallianwala Bagh as part of her regular visit to the Golden Temple. Now the public garden housed a memorial to commemorate the massacre of peaceful protestors and celebrants including unarmed men, women and children by soldiers of the then British rulers in 1919.

The guide was telling the Indian tourists, "This memorial is of national importance in the history of Indian independence from the

British. Around one thousand five hundred innocent Indians died and many were injured on the day of the Sikh festival of Vaisakhi on the 13th of April 1919. Indians of all faiths including Sikhs, Hindus and Muslims lost their lives on this day. It marked the turning point in the end of the British rule in India."

Jasmeet walked slowly to the water well and the place where her father had fallen. She could feel her heart hammering in her chest. She knelt in front of the bullet marks on the wall. There was a sign on the wall that one hundred and twenty men, women and children had been found dead in the well. People jumped into the well to escape the hail of gunfire. Parents had died trying to shield their children and as she read those words, tears streamed down her cheeks as she relived how her father had shielded her.

For years afterwards, she had been terrified of coming back here, taking longer routes around her city to avoid being near Jallianwalla Bagh. She'd been raised by her grandfather who had given her everything, but every day she remembered watching her parents being killed in front of her. Anger and fear had dominated the rest of her childhood, alleviated only by pride at every demonstration and protest she'd seen against the British as she'd grown up. Every day, she saw fresh waves of arrests as the soldiers tried to impose more and more restrictions, but this didn't dampen her spirit.

As she became older, she became emboldened to join the protests herself, inspired by the fighting spirit of those around her and the dream of freedom. She saw the movement against the British grow, and slowly laws started to be repealed around the censorship of the press, the powers of the police to detain without charge, and the freedom to protest as India worked towards independence. Never again did she want to see her country imprisoned and degraded in the way she had witnessed as child. And yet, despite her spirit, and her determination to ensure her parents' lives were not lost in vain, never before had she been able to return to Jallianwalla Bagh.

As she stared at the ground where she'd lost her parents, Jasmeet felt her grandchild's hand reach into hers and squeeze tightly, just as she'd held on to her Papa.

"Why you crying, Grandma?"

"These tears are for my parents, who sacrificed their lives for me."

And tears ran down Pinky's cheeks as she prayed for three small children and their parents.

4

With everyone gone, the house felt empty. Too often these days, Pinky couldn't stem her tears. Then she thought of Bobby's words to her on the morning of that fateful day.

When I look back at my life, I have no regrets. I met my best friend in my wife, my soulmate.

Remembering how she'd met Bobby brought a smile to her face. She'd been sixteen years old. Her father, a major in the Indian army, knew Bobby's grandfather.

He invited them to their village in Punjab so Bobby could meet Pinky with a view to marriage.

Bobby had often described driving into the village.

The green trees were surrounded by the mustard crop with yellow blossoms. It seemed a bright yellow carpet was spread all around. Cows mooed, birds chirped. Romance was in the air.

Pinky had been playing with her friends on the colourful swings attached by a rope to the branch of a large tree. The girls were singing and laughing.

Peacocks with colourful feathers, green, yellow, blue, red and gold, spread like a rainbow in the sky, danced in the rain.

The girls pushed Pinky's swing, harder and harder.

She shouted, "I feel like a bird, flying in the sky."

A young man approached. "I have come to visit Major Sahib. Where is his house?"

The girls giggled and pointed to Pinky. "She's Major's daughter."

Pinky jumped down from her swing and ran through the fields as fast as she could. Puffing and panting, she entered the back door of the house.

She was told that Bobby had come to see her so she needed to take in tea and snacks for the guests.

Carrying fried pakoras, samosas, sweet gulab jamun and jalebi, as per the Indian custom on such occasions, Pinky entered the sitting room. Her father introduced her. Bobby's grandfather asked her to sit next to Bobby on the settee.

After taking tea, Bobby asked Pinky's father for permission to talk to her privately. Outside the house, they stood under a magnolia tree.

He began, "I saw you flying like a bird. Your electrifying smile lit your eyes like the stars in the sky. Will you marry me?"

"Ask my father," she'd replied. Then she ran back to the house.

How unromantic! Bobby later reported thinking.

But Major and Bobby's grandfather were already celebrating the engagement.

5

One morning, Seema rang. "How are you, Pinky?"

"I feel only despair and despondency. I don't feel like meeting people or getting out of the house."

"I'm coming to see you today."

Seema convinced Pinky to accompany her to their favourite hotel for high tea.

Sitting in the majestic tea room, Pinky confided, "Sometimes, I see Bobby in a red car with lights on outside my house. When I go out, there is no car. Why doesn't he come in? Is he angry with me?"

"It is an illusion. You miss Bobby so much that your mind is playing tricks. You must focus on the good memories where you and Bobby used to laugh together. This will help your mind."

"We used to laugh together a lot," conceded Pinky.

"I'd love to hear about it."

"OK. I will tell you a story from my life in India after our marriage. My father introduced Bobby to the young village clinic doctor, Jeevan. Over time, they became good friends. One day, Bobby asked him what attracted him to a village clinic when he could earn much more in the city. This was his reply about what happened when he was a medical intern in the city hospital.

One day, a nurse shouted for the doctor, saying the patient in bed 15 was having a fit. In I came, running. I'd only recently graduated and this was my second week working as an intern in the medical ward. It was 3 o'clock in the morning. Lying motionless in bed 15, the patient called Babu was not breathing. I placed my stethoscope on the patient's chest. No heart sounds. I checked the patient's eyes with the torch. The pupils were dilated and fixed. With great sadness, I certified death and closed the curtains around the bed.

A half an hour or so had passed when the nurse came back, to move the dead patient. She opened the curtains and screamed in horror. Sitting on the bed and staring at her was Babu.

Babu got up from the bed. The nurse fell on the floor. She'd fainted. When the other nurses saw Babu trying to lift her up, they were shocked. They looked in astonishment. Babu was calling for help but the nurses weren't moving, frozen where they stood.

The nurse in charge helped the nurse on the floor to get up. She called the medical consultant.

When told about the wrong death certification, he summoned me. "Dr Jeevan, you idiot! Last week, you were checking the chest of a breathless patient and told me you couldn't hear any breath sounds. I checked your stethoscope, it was not opened. I rotated the chest piece and you said you could hear the breath sounds now. Is it possible that the chest piece of your stethoscope may have been closed again? The patient is a cocaine addict. His pupils would have been dilated but not fixed and would have reacted to torchlight. This is a serious medical error."

The nurse in charge said, "Thank God I hadn't informed the family."

The consultant was angry with me for my negligence in confirming the death of the patient but he did not want to ruin my career.

He told me, "If I report you to the authorities, you will be suspended. Our villages need doctors. If you promise to work in rural areas after finishing your internship, I will withhold my complaint."

Of course, I agreed.

'Bobby started calling him, "My idiot friend but a good doctor to all except those who are dying." Even after coming to UK, we'd laugh every time Bobby remembered Dr Jeevan.'

Seema hooted with laughter, while Pinky thanked Seema for the high tea and making her feel better.

Seema noted that Pinky had eaten very little. She used to love these cakes.

6

A few days later, Seema visited again.

When Pinky talked about her loss of interest in food, she convinced her to see the family doctor.

With Pinky's permission, Seema accompanied her to the consultation. Seema asked her to start with seeing Bobby in a car outside her home.

"Doctor, I see my husband in a red car with lights on outside my house. When I go out, there is no car. I don't know what's happening."

Seema interrupted. "Her husband, Bobby, died recently."

"I am sorry to hear that."

The doctor continued, "What time of day do you see Bobby?"

"Usually evenings."

"How is your sleep?"

"Disturbed. I get up in the early hours every night and then cannot go back to sleep."

"What thoughts do you have at night?"

"I cry a lot. Thoughts of why I am alive when Bobby has died. Life is not worth living."

"Any suicidal thoughts?"

"Yes. Sometimes."

"Have you ever acted on these thoughts?"

"Sorry, what do you mean?"

"Any self-harm?" asked the doctor.

"No."

"How is your appetite?"

"I don't feel like eating anymore but I used to enjoy food."

The doctor told Pinky seeing Bobby was a visual hallucination, likely due to depression in her bereavement. He prescribed antidepressants and reassured her that as her depression lifted, poor sleep and appetite would also improve.

"I am referring you to a clinical psychologist to help you with depression and bereavement."

7

Mornings were difficult. Pinky did not want to get out of bed.

Bobby has left me. Mother died many years ago. Father also died in a car accident some years ago. I had no siblings. No one is left. No one loves me. Why live?

She thought *if she had children, there would have been love in the house.*

She had undergone three IVF procedures without success. Bobby did not agree to adoption of a child.

Surrogacy was their last resort.

They approached a surrogacy clinic in India. Babita was to be the surrogate mother.

She worked as a servant in Mumbai.

She earned Rs 6000 a month (£60). Her husband was an ill-natured, hot tempered, unemployed alcoholic who was only interested in the money Babita earned.

They lived in one room in a sprawling Mumbai slum. The living conditions were squalid and miserable. Every day was filled with struggle for basic things, water scarcity and lack of toilets while rich people lived in big houses next to the slum area.

Babita thought, *Our hard work makes the life of rich people comfortable while we struggle so much.*

Despite her bleak life, she was blissful. "We should thank God for whatever life he has gifted us."

One day, an agent for a surrogacy clinic approached her. "Listen, sister, would you like to earn Rs 100,000 (£1000)?"

"I am a devout person. I would not do any sinful work even if I were dying of hunger," replied Babita.

"No, sister, it is not sinful at all. You would be helping childless couples."

"I have two boys and one girl of my own. I sympathise with the suffering of people who cannot have children but tell me, what is involved?"

"You will never meet the parents. You carry their fertilised egg in your womb. After delivery, the baby is given to the intended parents."

"How is it possible?"

"The specialist doctor implants the embryo which he has developed in his laboratory between the sperm of man and egg of his wife."

"Could I see the baby after birth and meet the intended parents?" asked Babita.

"You could not, you would have to abide by the agreement. I could introduce you to a woman, who is a surrogate mother. She lives in your colony. She has been a surrogate twice, earning Rs 200,000 in total."

"My God, that is a lot of money for being pregnant," exclaimed Babita.

She met the surrogate mother, who called it an act of kindness, "Giving happiness to a childless couple."

She told her husband about the surrogacy and the money

earned but told him only Rs 30,000 in case he had ideas of spending it all on alcohol.

He readily agreed, thinking he could drink whisky instead of cheap Indian booze.

Babita hoped the money would help in her children's education. She started attending the private fertility clinic. She underwent a battery of tests. She was given medications and injections. The doctor explained that this was to prepare her body for the embryo's transfer to her womb.

Then, the day came when the doctor and the nurse took her to the operating theatre and the embryo was implanted into her uterus. It was successful.

Her pregnancy was uneventful.

When she was about seven months pregnant, her husband came home drunk.

"Give me money," he demanded.

"I don't have any."

"I know you have Rs 30,000."

"No, they will only pay me when I have the baby."

"You're lying," he snarled.

He was tall and muscular. She was petite.

"You can ask the doctor," said Babita, frightened.

He slapped her. "You fool me by acting religious but you are a sinner. An evil person. The baby in a womb carries the soul of God. You should be ashamed of yourself."

She reported the incident to the doctor.

The doctor was concerned. "We can move you to a safe hostel for women."

"But I have three children aged 2,3 and 5 years old."

"They are all quite young," said the doctor.

"Yes, which is fortunate because my 5 year old is already asking questions about my big tummy."

The doctor agreed for Babita to stay at home but insisted

that if she faced any risk of domestic violence, she would have to move.

She told her husband, "If you hit me and I lose the baby, we will not get any money."

He apologised and promised to behave himself.

Babita thought, *sometimes even the desire of alcohol can have a sobering effect.*

One night, she started having pains. She phoned the doctor. He sent her an ambulance for the delivery suite of a private hospital. The midwives sedated her so that the baby could be removed immediately after birth, without her seeing the baby.

Despite that, she managed to regain full consciousness and refused to let her baby be taken away.

"This little girl is my baby. Nine months of bonding and baby kicks inside me."

"You are in pain. The doctor will give you medication for pain and suppressing your breastmilk," advised the midwife.

"No, this breast milk is for my baby. Not to be suppressed," shouted Babita in anger.

"You won't get any money. The agency will take you to court. Please think again."

"I will fight for my baby until my last breath," she told the midwives. "I know I signed an agreement that I would not have any interaction with the baby and the intended parents but it is wrong, morally wrong," she told the solicitor who approached her.

The solicitor threatened her with court proceedings and told her she would lose in court.

Devastated, Pinky and Bobby had a dilemma whether to stay in India to fight the court case which could last many years or return to England. Bobby's shoe factory was struggling and would fail without Bobby working in Bradford.

Meeting Babita, Bobby gave her a signed empty cheque for her to fill in any amount she wanted. She was not interested and returned the cheque.

Crying, Pinky begged her for the baby but to no avail.

Returning empty handed was traumatic, but Bobby reassured Pinky, "We have each other and our love. If this is God's Will, who are we to question? We have to accept it."

Pinky was a religious person who believed that whatever happens in life, happens for a purpose. Over time, she accepted it. Her life was filled with Bobby's love.

8

It was appointment day. Despite her nerves, Pinky reached the hospital in time.

A young clinical psychologist led her to her room. "I am sorry to hear about your husband. Please do tell me about your worries."

"I feel low and weepy. I talk loudly to myself all day. I am embarrassed."

"What do you talk about loudly? What are your thoughts?"

"I cannot help but repeat all day that I am horrible and no one loves me."

"Any other self-talk?"

"I let my husband down. It is all my fault. My life gets worse every day. Bad things always happen to me. I don't like anything about myself. I am a disaster, disgusting and dangerous."

The psychologist asked more questions, including about the red car.

At the end of the consultation, she reassured Pinky that there was no evidence of a serious mental illness. She agreed with the family doctor that Pinky was experiencing a combination of bereavement and depression. Pinky talking to herself might also be a symptom of anxiety disorder.

She told Pinky that she would send her an appointment for counselling sessions but in the meantime, she advised her to write her thoughts in a diary. "I want you to be aware of all your thoughts and replace them with constructive thoughts. These thoughts are not true but imaginary fears because our evolution of brain is wired to look for dangers. You can help yourself by writing in your diary three things you are grateful for every day."

"I cannot think of any such things," said Pinky.

The psychologist asked her about her life with Bobby. Was there anything to celebrate?

"Oh yes. A very happy long married life of 57 years. I married him aged 16 years. I am lucky and blessed to have had a husband like Bobby."

The psychologist said if she could repeat aloud many times a day, *I am lucky, I am blessed*, that would train the mind to cancel the negative thoughts.

Pinky thanked the psychologist and left.

9

One day, there was a knock on the door. It was Paul.

"What a surprise," said Pinky.

"I have taken a gap year in my studies, so I decided to visit you."

"Welcome, Paul."

At lunch, Pinky informed him that she had a psychologist appointment that afternoon.

"How come you're seeing a psychologist?" asked Paul.

"My doctor referred me. I started seeing a red car with Bobby outside the house."

"And are you better?"

"The psychologist feels that I am suffering with depression and anxiety. I will need counselling sessions to get better."

Alone at home that afternoon, Paul started going through Bobby's personal possessions. After about an hour, he found what he was looking for. The two wills. Both were mirror wills, leaving everything to each other.

"When the surviving partner dies, the estate will pass to Jasmeet, Bobby's sister," read the will.

How disgusting. Me and Dad live in UK but Bobby has given everything to his sister in India!

Paul rang his dad, Ranjit.

"Dad, you are not a benefactor in the will. Why did Bobby treat you so unjustly?"

Ranjit was angry. He explained that when he came to England, he thought Bobby was helping him by giving him a job in his shoe factory, but it turned out to be sheer exploitation with long hours and poor pay. When he complained, Bobby reminded him that food and living in the house was free. "Who pays his elder bother for food and accommodation? Besides, there was always criticism of my work. Once, he insulted me in front of the other factory workers. Enough was enough. I decided to take my rightful pay from the cash box whenever I could. One day, he caught me redhanded. Told me that he was doing me a favour by not reporting to the police. After calling me a thief, he sacked me."

"'You bastard. You greedy, selfish man. You should be ashamed of yourself,' I shouted at him. Since then, we haven't talked to each other. But now I will take my due."

10

Hovering outside Pinky's room with tea, toast and fried eggs, Paul heard talking and a loud laughter.

Slowly opening the door, he found Pinky alone.

"Sorry for not knocking. I heard you talking and then laughing. I thought you were on your mobile ..."

"I do talk to myself aloud sometimes."

"How come you were laughing?" asked Paul.

"Memories are weird. You laugh, despite feeling dark and chaotic. The psychologist wants me to think and write down all the funny and humorous memories where I and Bobby used to laugh together. One such memory from India came back to me."

"What happened?" asked Paul.

Pinky narrated the story.

It is the story of Bobby's friend Satish.

The bridegroom, Satish, was woken by a knock on his bedroom door. He got up from the bed with some difficulty. He staggered to open the door.

"It's past 12 noon, you never get up so late," said his mother.

"Sorry, I am not feeling well. I am feeling dizzy and drowsy."

"Where is your wife?"

"Maybe in the bath?"

"There is no one in your bathroom," replied his mother, after looking around. "Oh look, there's a handwritten note."

"What does it say?"

"I am leaving you and your city of Kanpur. Please don't look for me and do not report my disappearance to the police."

Satish was shocked out of his drowsiness. The safe in his bedroom was open. He had put all the money, gifted by friends and relatives, in the safe last night. He remembered locking it and putting the key in his pocket.

His mother screamed. "She has taken all the cash and gold jewellery. She was a thief."

Satish rubbed his eyes. "Is this a bad dream? It can't be true."

Yesterday, he was the bridegroom on horseback. There was the wedding band in front of him and all his friends and relatives dancing behind him.

His mind wandered back to his advertisement on the matrimonial page of the national newspaper of India.

Handsome, 5'9" Hindu aged 29 years, MBA, manager at a multinational company seeks a beautiful, educated girl. Caste no bar.

The next day, he had received a phone call. "Hello, I want to talk about the matrimonial advertisement."

"Sure, I am Satish. I placed that advertisement."

"Oh, good. I am a businessman in London. Kanta is my beautiful daughter. She is a graduate from a university in England. She is proud of her Indian heritage and desires an arranged marriage with an Indian. Can we meet?"

"Yes, where?"

"I am staying in the hotel Sherbet. If you come tomorrow at 6 p.m., me and Kanta can see you."

"Sure."

Satish with his mother met Kanta and her father.

Kanta bowed and touched the feet of his mother respectfully.

Satish thought, here is a girl educated in England, who is steeped in the Indian culture of showing respect for elders.

She had green eyes and wore a green bindi on her forehead. She was 5' 9" tall with fair complexion. She wore a silk green sari, which she carried gracefully in a confident manner.

Satish whispered, "You look amazing."

She replied, "Thanks."

Time flew so quickly and they had so much to talk about, that it was soon 10 p.m.

They had dinner together and agreed to meet soon.

Next morning, Kanta's father telephoned Satish. "You will be pleased to know that my daughter liked you. What are your thoughts regarding her and marriage?"

He was taken aback by the speed of the proposal but he did find Kanta very attractive.

He replied, "Ummm yes."

Next morning at their house, there was an elderly man, wearing a bright yellow robe, gold-rimmed glasses and a long red bead necklace. Kanta's father introduced him as a learned astrologer. He asked Satish, "What is the date and time of your birth?"

"I can give my date of birth but I need to ask my mum for the time of birth."

His mum replied, "It was after midnight."

The astrologer asked, "Can you give me the exact time? The more accurate, the better my prediction for a happy marriage."

She replied, "It was a few minutes after midnight."

"OK, let me study the alignment of stars and planets relating to the

birth of both Satish and Kanta. Oh, good news, it would be a marriage made in heaven but you would have to tie the knot within one week."

Satish felt that the marriage date was too early. His mother, a strong believer in astrology, convinced her son to agree.

"I don't have time to arrange funds from London. I'll pay you when the funds arrive. In the meantime, you organise the wedding and make all the payments," said Kanta's father.

"Sure, Sir," replied Satish.

Satish's mother was unhappy. "In India, the bride's father pays for all wedding expenses."

"Don't worry, he said he will return all the money soon," replied Satish.

Satish took some time off work and worked frantically to arrange the venue and wedding services. There was so much to arrange at such short notice. The invitation cards really tired him, he was hand-delivering them right up until the wedding day. All his tiredness disappeared when Kanta stepped onto the decorated dais wearing a flashy red sari. She was decked out with gold jewellery. She had red bindi designs on her forehead. Her long hair was tied in a flower-wrapped bun. She looked stunning and glamorous, though she was very quiet during the marriage ceremony.

Homecoming with Kanta was great. The post-wedding rituals of welcoming the bride to her marital home were carried out at the door. Kanta gently pushed the pot filled with rice towards the house with her right leg to bring prosperity and fortune to her new home.

On entering the house, she said, "I'm not feeling well. I need some sleep."

He woke her up at 9 p.m. "Have something to eat, please."

"I don't feel like eating but I will drink milk if you join me," replied Kanta.

Satish thought that Kanta was not used to Indian rituals and the stress had got to her.

He thought, I will keep her happy. I will be a caring husband. She will get used to life in India.

That's the last conversation he remembers.

Satish told his mother, "She probably drugged my milk. Don't tell anyone, it is very embarrassing."

"You have to inform the police. Most of the jewellery was given to me by my late mother. We have to recover it."

He visited the local police station and filed a First Information Report.

The police officer asked, "Can you provide her photograph?"

"Sure, I will get my marriage photographs from the photographer."

Then he remembered Kanta's father had told him, "You don't have to spend money on photography and videography, it is my friend's business and he has offered to provide the service free of charge." There'd been no trace of this photographer.

However, thanks to one of his friends, a trainee photographer, Satish provided police with their marriage photograph. The local police circulated the photos to the police of every state in India.

After two weeks, there was a call from the police station. "We wanted to inform you that we have arrested Kanta and her father. They were caught crossing the Indian border into Nepal."

"What a strange story. Did they recover the cash and jewellery?" asked Paul.

"No, nothing was recovered. Satish never married again. When Bobby used to ring him from England, he used to say, 'I am your friend, not a marriage scammer. I will go on teasing you until you get married again.'"

11

Paul phoned his dad.

"She attends psychology sessions in the hospital."

"Why?"

"She sees Bobby in a red car. She talks to herself and constantly laughs aloud."

"She is mad. Gain her trust and ask her to transfer the estate to you," said Ranjit.

Paul started helping Pinky in cooking, washing utensils and cleaning the house.

"You're spoiling me," Pinky would say, as he served breakfast in her bedroom.

"I promised Bobby I'd look after you."

"I fear I wouldn't be able to cope without you now. You do everything for me," Pinky sighed.

One day, Pinky broke her glasses. Having problems with vision, Paul took her to the optician. Pinky was surprised when he brought two pairs of glasses, saying, "If one breaks, no problem."

She prepared to pay but he refused.

Pinky said, "I can never forget Bobby's words in hospital, 'You are our son. We are blessed to have you.'"

"And I am blessed to have you as my mother," said Paul, as tears welled up in her eyes.

12

Next morning, a loud noise woke Paul.

It was coming from Pinky's room. "I am horrible. No one loves me."

She was shouting this again and again.

Paul knocked on the door. "Everything OK?"

No reply, so he entered.

Pinky was slumped at the head of the bed amongst the pillows. Her gaze rose to meet Paul's when he entered, but seemed fixed on something behind him, watery and distant.

"Are you OK?"

"Sorry, can't hear you. Let me get my hearing aid."

"Are you OK, Pinky?"

"Yes, I can hear you now. Thanks."

Tears rolled down her cheeks.

"I feel so lonely without Bobby. I feel no one loves me."

"Don't say that. Paul, your son, loves you very much."

She hugged him.

"Can I offer some advice, if you don't mind?"

"Sure."

"Your antidepressants and counselling aren't helping. I know a private psychiatrist who can help. Can I make you an appointment?"

A week before the psychiatrist appointment, Paul convinced her to sign a power of attorney at the lawyer's office. The forms were signed by both Pinky and the solicitor.

In the forms, Pinky declared, "I am capable of making the decision for myself," in front of the solicitor. Paul Kohli was named the appointed attorney in the legal document.

"This is going to protect you from any problems in life," Paul assured her.

13

Next day was the appointment day with the psychiatrist in a private hospital.

When Pinky got up in the morning, she couldn't find her hearing aid. "Without it, I'll have difficulty hearing the psychiatrist."

"Don't worry, I'll help you," said Paul. "Don't be late for the appointment."

The receptionist ushered them to the psychiatrist's office.

"Before I start my consultation, do you give your permission for Paul to attend the consultation?" asked the psychiatrist.

Looking at Paul, Pinky saw him nodding and did the same.

Paul explained that Pinky had hearing problems but she could lip-read.

The psychiatrist read her booking-in form.

"Name, Pinky Kohli. Age 73, a widow sees Bobby, her deceased husband, in a red car outside her house many times a day."

Paul explained that she went outside to bring him in each

time but he refused, telling her that he'd remarried and she should forget him now.

"Is that true, Pinky?" asked the psychiatrist.

She nodded, without understanding.

Paul went on, "She wanders outside and doesn't know where she is. I have to keep the door locked at all times for her safety. She talks to herself and laughs without any reason."

"How is her appetite?"

"She goes on asking for more food as she forgets that she's already eaten."

"How is her sleep?"

"She will get up in the middle of night and wander about the house. A few times, she almost caused a fire as she put on the gas at night and forgot. I now lock the kitchen."

Memory testing for cognitive assessment was confusing for Pinky.

After blood tests were taken, Paul gave his email for the psychiatrist to send the diagnosis and treatment plan.

After a few days, the psychiatrist's email arrived.

Diagnosis: Alzheimer's.

Paul rang Ranjit. "We're winning. She has been diagnosed with dementia."

"Well done, son. You're a gem."

14

One morning, Seema dropped in.

"I've been ringing but there was no reply. I got worried."

"I lost my hearing aids so didn't hear my mobile. Today, Paul kindly got me new hearing aids," replied Pinky.

She told Seema about the psychiatrist appointment without her hearing aid.

"That's not right. You should have cancelled," replied Seema.

"Paul advised me that I can manage as he would help me. I just nodded without understanding the questions."

"Why did you not speak up and tell the psychiatrist you weren't understanding?" asked Seema.

"I don't know. I just trusted Paul. Also last week, I signed lots of papers with Paul at the office."

"Which office and what papers?"

"I don't know. Paul told me that they were for my protection. Was I wrong to sign?"

"You used to be mentally sharp, alert and careful. You don't seem to be mentally clear now. Can I make an appointment with your family doctor? I can come with you and help you to explain."

Seema rang the doctor's surgery and made an appointment.

Paul was upstairs listening to Seema's talk with Pinky. He shouldn't have let her in. He'd have to stop her, somehow, before she got too involved.

15

After Seema had left, Paul ordered Pinky's favourite takeaway.

Sitting for lunch, Pinky was quiet.

"Anything worrying you?" asked Paul.

"Seema thinks I am not mentally clear. I did not know what papers I had signed."

"I promised Bobby I'd look after you. Whatever I do is to protect you. After Bobby, you are more precious to me than anyone."

She burst into tears

"Bobby told you to be strong. Believe me, I'll never let you down," reassured Paul.

"You are my son. I trust you."

Paul managed to get Pinky's mobile while she was in the prayer room. It was lying on the bed, open and unlocked.

He sent a message to her doctor's surgery cancelling her appointment.

Then he sent a message to Seema.

> You are interfering in my life. I wish to grieve in peace without any extra pressure from you. Please do not ring me or visit. I don't want any stress from you.

After about an hour, the doorbell rang.

Paul looked outside. Standing at the door was Seema.

He ran upstairs to check on Pinky. He was relieved to find that Pinky was in the bath, her mobile ringing on her bed. When he saw it was Seema calling, he grabbed up the mobile. He threw it from the top of the stairs a few times until it stopped functioning.

Instead of returning the mobile to her bed, he put it on floor next to the bed as if it had fallen.

When he came back downstairs, Seema had left.

He rang his dad, describing the narrow escape.

16

Checking the post, Paul was glad to see the registered power of attorney papers for Pinky.

He was the appointed attorney for everything including finance, property, health and welfare.

As Pinky was declared to be suffering with Alzheimer's, he didn't need her permission to sell her property.

That night, Paul did his research.

Bobby and Pinky had two properties besides their home. If he sold them, he could make around two million pounds.

Pinky's savings in the bank stood at about £500,000. As an appointed attorney, he could withdraw as much cash as needed from Pinky's savings, gifting money to himself and to his dad.

If she died, his attorney authority would be cancelled.

He compiled a list of nursing and care homes.

Next morning, he contacted the care homes as they were cheaper than nursing homes.

He found one in the outskirts of Bradford. It was a struggling care home with poor reviews.

The owner was bit reluctant. "We don't provide dementia care. We have no nurses."

When Paul insisted he'd pay extra, the owner agreed.

Paul insisted that no guests including her family and friends would be permitted to see Pinky. Also, he would deliver the prescription medicines himself.

The owner said, "I agree to your instructions provided all fees are paid on time. No exceptions."

17

"I've found a care home, but how do I convince her to agree? I'm frightened of over sedating her in case of complications."

Ranjit replied, "Bhang is your answer. Let me tell you a true story."

Ranjit narrated the story of Raju, a farm worker employed by his friend in an Indian border village.

It was Holi, the Indian festival of colour. It marks the arrival of spring and celebrates love as well as triumph of good over evil. The farm workers were throwing coloured powder known as gulal at each other. They made the Bhang lassi drink from yogurt and cannabis, ground and mixed with water. Raju knew it was a funny intoxicant. It gives some people fits of uncontrollable laughter; others of bottomless melancholy. He was reluctant to take it.

His friend Chotu said, "Come on, it is Holi today, you have to take Bhang. In the village, we always celebrated Holi by drinking Bhang."

Chotu gave Raju a big glass of Bhang drink. Raju started drinking, cheered on by other farm workers.

He was soon as high as a kite. He felt the clouds floating down towards him – or was it he who was floating up? As if in a mist, he saw his friend. He went forward to wish him Happy Holi but all he could manage was a continuous stream of laughter. The friend smeared his face with colours and he went on laughing.

Then, tears rolled down his cheeks. He was inconsolable.

"Why are you crying?"

"I miss my sisters," replied Raju, wandering away.

"Where are you going?" asked Chotu.

"To play Holi with my sisters. Look, I grabbed a couple of packets of coloured powder and put them in my pockets. I will throw colours at my sisters and they'll drench me with coloured water."

"Sure, sure, do that," said Chotu, laughing loudly. "You will have to walk one thousand miles all the way to your village in Bihar, on your unsteady feet."

"Yes, yes, I'll walk all the way."

He walked into the darkness. Then, he stumbled but got up and started singing, "It is Holi today. Let's drink and be merry."

"Halt, halt or we shoot!" The powerful light blinded him. He froze. When he managed to open his eyes, he had been pushed to the ground and both his hands were handcuffed. They were frisking his body thoroughly. "Any weapons on you?"

Raju looked up and saw soldiers with guns pointing at him.

"I am Indian, I am Indian, please don't shoot me."

"Are you an Indian spy? Why have you entered Pakistan?"

"Am I in Pakistan?"

"Don't act smart now, we know how to get the information from you."

"If this drink can make a poor farm worker cross the border and get imprisoned for many years, I am sure it will land Pinky in the care home," concluded Ranjit.

"Ok, send me this Bhang drink."

18

At the table having breakfast, Paul told Pinky, "You mentioned suffering with constipation. I contacted your doctor's surgery. They prescribed sachets to be taken in a drink before breakfast. I have made the drink as per their advice."

"I hope they help me."

Paul gave her the Bhang drink. "Drink it up straightaway."

"It tastes weird."

"You need to finish it."

After an hour, Pinky was sobbing uncontrollably. She looked confused and restless.

Paul contacted the residential care home and informed them that Pinky was on her way.

When she arrived, she was laughing hysterically.

Paul thought, *Bhang is a mysterious drink.*

The care assistant, Cath, led her to her room and asked Paul, "I've been told she has Alzheimer's. Does she get aggressive and violent? We're not trained to look after dementia sufferers."

"Oh not at all. She is pleasantly confused," replied Paul. "But do not permit any visitor, even if they claim they are friends or relatives. That is what upsets her, making her unpleasant and aggressive. Remember, no visitors at all."

Next morning, Pinky was drowsy but not confused. She shouted at the care workers, "I have been kidnapped. You are keeping me here against my will. I'll report you to the police."

The owner rang Paul to take her away as Pinky was disturbing the other residents.

Paul arrived and pacified Pinky. "This place is temporary. You'll go home soon."

He gave her double dose of the strong sedatives.

He reassured the owner, "I forgot to leave her medicine. She is well controlled on her medication. I promise you, I will supply her medication every month and there will be no problems."

Paul gave the sedatives to Cath with a double dose written on the medicine bottle. "Administer every morning, please."

19

Cath came back to work after her annual holiday. She asked her colleagues about Pinky.

"Pinky spends most of her time in her room. She's not happy here."

Cath suddenly remembered that before going on holiday, she'd forgotten to tell her colleagues the special instructions regarding Pinky's medication tablets.

Feeling guilty, Cath went straight to Pinky's room.

When she opened the door, Cath asked, "How are you, Pinky?"

"Not feeling well," replied Pinky.

"What happened?"

"No one loves me. No one comes to see me. I feel so lonely, so hopeless. My husband loved me but he died months ago."

Cath hugged her. "I'll be your friend."

She took her down to the dining room.

Most of the residents were English in their late eighties or nineties.

Pinky struggled to hold conversations with them.

Sitting down for dinner, Pinky was not enjoying the English food. She asked Cath, "Can I sometimes have Indian food?"

The care manager, Mrs Hamilton, walked in.

Cath told her about Pinky's request for Indian food sometimes.

"We can't make special food for one person," replied Mrs Hamilton.

"Well, it's not fair. You also refused me a mobile as mine was broken."

"We have instructions not to provide you with one."

"Why? From who?"

"I can't say."

"You arranged a minibus to the church on Sunday. When I requested if someone would take me to my temple, you refused. You always refuse my request. Why?"

"Because your requests are unreasonable," replied the care manager.

"It is your duty to look after me," said Pinky, raising her voice.

"Don't shout at me. I am not your servant. I know how you treat your servants in India," said the manager, walking away.

Pinky asked Cath, "Why did she say that?"

"I don't know. I'm sorry that she did," replied Cath, sitting beside Pinky. "I'm really sorry about all of this."

"It's not your fault. I respect you because you have compassion and empathy."

They walked back to Pinky's room.

With tears in her eyes, Pinky narrated a true story of a servant in the household of her uncle, Sajinder Singh Anand, in India.

Babulal came from a poor family in Bihar. When he was sixteen years old, he migrated to Punjab.

Mr Sajinder Anand employed him as a domestic servant.

Mrs Anand treated him like her son. He was fed well and allowed to watch his favourite programmes on their television set as his room did not have television. She taught him how to cook. When she made his favourite dish, he said, "You remind me of my mother."

Walking with the stick, Mrs Anand aged 81 told Babulal, "We will go to the vegetable and fruit market three times a week. They get everything fresh, especially seasonal fruits. Nowadays summer king of fruits, mangoes are available.

"Oh, I love mangoes," said Babulal.

"OK, mangoes for you every time we go to the market."

One day, Mrs Anand suddenly died after a heart attack. Sajinder was devastated. Babulal was grief-stricken.

A year passed by. Sajinder was losing weight and interest in playing golf, which was his love and passion. Every morning, Babulal used to take him to the golf club but now Mr Anand refused, complaining, "I wake up at 3 a.m. and then I am unable to go back to sleep."

Babulal said, "Sir, it would be a good exercise and you would enjoy playing and meeting friends."

"No, I don't want to go, I get very tired."

Babulal telephoned Maninder Anand, their only son, who lived in the same city about ten miles away.

"Sir, I am worried about your dad. He is losing weight, always tired, and he has even stopped going to the golf course."

"Since when?"

"Since about two months."

"Why did you not take him to the doctor?"

"I did. The doctor said Mr Anand is suffering with depression and gave him tablets but it is not helping."

"Why not see the doctor again?"

"He refused."

"OK, I'll come tomorrow and talk to him."

Maninder came and convinced his dad and they visited a

consultant physician. The physician ordered blood tests, scans and organised a camera test of Mr Anand's stomach.

One evening, the physician's secretary phoned. "The doctor wants to see Mr Anand with his son tomorrow at 9 a.m."

Next day, the physician announced, "Mr Anand, the results have come back."

"Yes, what is it?"

"I am sorry to say, you have stomach cancer."

"I knew something was seriously wrong with me."

"We need to get the tumour out. I have discussed with my surgical colleague and the stomach operation needs to be done urgently."

"When?"

"Soon."

"What's the prognosis?" asked Maninder.

"It is difficult to say at present."

During the journey home, everyone was quiet in the car.

Babulal sensed everything was not well at the doctor's.

At night, he asked Mr Anand, "Was everything OK at the clinic?"

"No, I have cancer. I am having a stomach operation. I don't know how long I have to live."

"I'll pray for your long life."

"I'd rather have a short good life," said Mr Anand.

Babulal could not sleep at night. Tears flooded his eyes. He prayed, "Oh God, please give my life to Mr Anand and save him from the cancer."

After the operation, Maninder and his wife moved in temporarily to their dad's house. Maninder organised nurses to look after his dad.

Mr Anand was struggling to eat or drink. Babulal would cook his favourite dishes and spend many hours feeding him.

As time went by, Mr Anand needed more support.

Babulal would sleep on the floor in his bedroom. Babulal would get up at night and change Mr Anand's bedsheets and clean him with love and affection, whenever he had bowel incontinence.

Mr Anand would be apologetic. "I'm sorry, Babulal."

"No sir, you are my father, given to me by God."

Mr Anand was tearful. "My own son and daughter in law make faces when they enter my room. I have heard them complaining about the smell."

Babulal hugged him. For him, serving Mr Anand was his religious duty. He revered him.

He would hold his hand and take him for walks in the garden. Every morning, he would take him to a riverside walk and push him in the wheelchair. Mr Anand loved feeding birds.

When he heard birds singing from the trees, Mr Anand would cheer up. "Babulal, guess which tree the bird is singing from?"

He would stop when he saw children flying colourful kites.

He told Babulal, "In my childhood, I used to fly kites from the rooftop of our house. My father bought kites with sharp strings which cut the strings of rival kites in the sky. Me and my father would laugh at the broken kites. Those were the happy days, I thought they would never end."

One day, Babulal organised a surprise party at home and cooked all the best dishes and invited Mr Anand's friends. When Mr Anand saw his childhood friends and his golf friends, he was excited and asked, surprised, "Babulal, how did you manage to contact my childhood friends?"

"I've learnt from you that where there's a will, there's a way," said Babulal.

All the friends drank whisky and chatted until late at night. Babulal put on bhangra music and the next moment, the old pals were dancing with walking sticks and one even with crutches held high in his hands!

When everyone had left, Mr Anand said, "Thank you Babulal, that was the best day of my life."

Slowly, his health deteriorated. He now needed twenty-four-hour supervision.

Babulal hardly slept. He looked after Mr Anand as if every minute was precious. His affection was palpable.

Even Maninder said, "Babulal, I don't know what I'd do without you."

One morning, Mr Anand was smiling. "I am in nirvana, I am contented, I am thankful to God for giving me a good life."

"What is nirvana?" asked Babulal.

"It is like heaven."

"Don't we go to heaven after death?" asked Babulal innocently.

"Heaven and hell are state of mind. If you are contented, you are already in heaven," replied Mr Anand.

He died that night.

Next day, people noticed Sajinder had a smile on his face.

They commented, "He died happy."

Babulal murmured, "He was in nirvana."

After a week of religious prayers in the house, Maninder called Babulal and gave him his salary of Rs 5000.

He said, "I intend to sell the house. Please vacate the servant quarters before the end of the month."

The lawyer, Mr Ramesh, a close friend of Sajinder, was listening to the conversation.

He said, "Maninder, I want to read out the will, your father's will."

"Sure," replied Maninder.

Removing the will from the sealed envelope, Ramesh started reading.

"This is my last will. I revoke all earlier wills. I am in sound mind, memory and understanding.

I appoint Mr K.Ramesh, my lawyer, as the executor of my will.

I declare that my estate should be divided in the following shares:

50% Mr Maninder Anand, my own son

50% Mr Dev Babulal, the son given to me by God. He looked after me so well and gave me love, happiness and dignity."

Maninder was furious. He shouted at Babulal, "You planned this, didn't you, you manipulative servant."

Babulal could scarcely believe what he was hearing.

"Get out of the house before I call the police, you horrible thief," screamed Maninder.

Mr Ramesh told Maninder, "Your father knew you would react in such a manner, so he made sure that half of his estate in the name of Babulal is registered in the court and I have the legal papers which he signed in my presence."

Maninder looked in anger at Ramesh and told him, "You, as a lawyer and executor of the will, conspired with the servant to defraud my father and me."

"Absolutely baseless allegation," said the lawyer.

Maninder shouted, "I will take you all to the courts." The front door banged behind him.

Cath wiped the tears from her eyes. "What a story, full of love and affection." For a moment, Cath wondered if Pinky really did suffer from dementia. But she had seen her laughing uncontrollably without any reason on her first day at the care home. *I'm not a nurse or a doctor. How would I know?*

Cath told Pinky, "I forgot to tell my colleagues before I went on holidays that you should be given tablets every morning. Did you have any?"

"No."

"Sorry, my mistake. From tomorrow, you will be restarted on two tablets every morning."

20

One day, there was a knock on Pinky's door. Opening the door, she was glad to see Paul.

"Have you come to take me home?" she asked.

"Your house is still being repaired."

"Why, what happened to my home?"

"Don't you remember? Your house was severely damaged in a storm. How can you forget, Aunty? You woke to find the roof of your house blown away. The garden trees fell, damaging the wall which collapsed. Must have been terrifying for you."

Pinky was confused. *Am I going mad? I have no recollection of this storm.*

When she met Cath, Pinky confided in her. "I don't know what's happening to me. I forgot a big storm damage to my house. I woke up to find the roof of my house blown away but still cannot remember it. I had no memory problems before Bobby's death."

"Don't worry, love," Cath reassured her, thinking, *I've heard that in Alzheimer's, people have good and bad days. Maybe today is a bad day for Pinky.*

21

Four a.m. Screams were coming from Pinky's room.

Her neighbour knocked on her door. No reply. She called the night carer.

"What's wrong?"

"Tummy pains."

The ambulance arrived after about twenty minutes.

Examining her abdomen, the paramedic asked, "Where's the pain?"

"All over. I don't know."

"Any chest pain?"

"No."

The paramedic checked her heart, pulse, blood pressure and temperature. "Can I give you a morphine injection for the pain?"

Pinky nodded.

LYING IN THE SPEEDING AMBULANCE, WATCHING THROUGH

the window the top of houses and trees floating by, Pinky suddenly vomited.

After cleaning her, the paramedic checked her blood pressure again. "Don't worry. There's no blood in the vomitus. It's probably a side effect of morphine," the paramedic reassured her.

The ambulance reached the Accident and Emergency department of the hospital, and Pinky was taken in the stretcher.

A bed was ready in the emergency ward.

The paramedic shared her medical notes with the nurse at the hospital.

The nurse took the full medical history and then checked Pinky's pulse, blood pressure, temperature, and started an intravenous drip.

"How is your pain in the abdomen now, on a scale of one to ten?"

"Seven," replied Pinky.

The nurse offered paracetamol in the intravenous infusion, explaining, "It works faster through the drip."

Pinky agreed. The nurse left a vomit bag in case of need.

A short while later, Pinky vomited a profuse amount.

The nurse came running.

"Blood in your vomit. I'll call the doctor as soon as I've checked your pulse and blood pressure."

The doctor was soon checking Pinky.

"Your blood tests show that you are anaemic. Maybe you are losing blood. What colour is your poo?" asked the doctor.

"I don't know," replied Pinky. "What colour suggests blood?"

"Black," replied the doctor.

22

On the medical ward next morning, Pinky was trembling and sweating.

The nurse checked her temperature and called the doctor.

"Any pains?"

"Tummy pains," replied Pinky.

"Urinary problems?"

"No."

The doctor checked her lungs, heart and abdomen. All observations were normal

"Show me what medication you've been taking?"

"I left it in the care home."

At that moment, Paul arrived and Pinky introduced him to the doctor as her son.

"I need to see what medicines Pinky has been taking and a repeat prescription of her regular medication," said the doctor.

Paul smiled. "I've brought you the tablets she takes and a repeat prescription from her doctor."

"Good, show me."

The doctor looked at the tablets and the repeat prescription.

"These antidepressants are mild. They should not cause these withdrawal symptoms but can affect some patients. We'll keep an eye on her."

Over the next few days, Pinky was irritable, restless and felt weak.

Despite regular painkillers, her tummy pains persisted.

The gastroenterology consultant arranged a gastroscopy.

He explained to Pinky, "Gastroscopy is a type of endoscopy. A long, thin, flexible tube with a small camera inside will be put into your mouth, down your throat and into your stomach. If I see any abnormal or suspicious areas, I'll collect a biopsy during the procedure. It won't be painful, though you may experience some discomfort."

"Why a biopsy?" asked Pinky.

"We send the biopsy to the laboratory to check for cancer cells."

Pinky shuddered.

23

With an anaesthetic spray to the throat, the gastroenterologist introduced the tube with the camera. After about twenty minutes, the procedure complete, the consultant told Pinky, "I'm sending the biopsy samples to the laboratory."

"How long will the results take?"

"A few days, sometimes longer," replied the consultant.

Pinky endured a sleepless night.

On a ward round next evening, the gastroenterologist checked her abdomen.

"It looks swollen."

On examination, he found fluid in her abdomen.

"Is it normal to have fluid in the tummy?" asked Pinky.

"It is called ascites; fluid abdomen is abnormal. I'll order an ultrasound tomorrow morning."

The next day, the consultant sat with Pinky. "I'm sorry. The biopsy result showed cancer. The ultrasound showed ascites. We'll need to start treatment soon. The success rate is seventy percent."

"And if I'm in the thirty percent, how long do I have to live?" asked Pinky.

"I'm referring you to the oncologist. He is a cancer specialist. You are in good hands."

As she lay on her bed, staring on the ward ceiling, Pinky felt lonely and helpless. She thought of Bobby. *He would have nursed me back to health and an escape from this endless pain. My tears would have been wiped away, and laughter returned to our lovely life together.*

Feeling the gentle squeeze of a warm hand, Pinky looked up.

It was the nurse, Caroline. "You'll be alright. We're here to help you."

Pinky told her about Bobby. "I wish he'd come back to life."

"No one ever returns after death," said Caroline

"Oh yes, they do." And Pinky told Caroline the true story from India narrated to her by her father's friend Jogi, a journalist.

The man who rose from the dead in India.

No heart sounds, no eye reflexes, pupils fixed and dilated. As the doctor found no signs of life, he declared him dead.

His wife was wailing. Walking into the emergency department of the hospital, was Baba with his followers. The holy man covered the face of the dead man with both his hands and whispered something in his ears, followed by massaging his arms and legs.

Baba seemed to be praying now.

Was the dead man moving his legs? Oh yes, he was opening his eyes also.

People shouted, "Long live Babaji, our living God. Greatest in the world."

Baba was an elderly man with long hair and a long flowing white beard. He wore a yellow robe and wooden footwear. Rumour was, that Baba for many years lived and meditated in the Himalayan caves. He had a vision of God and decided to serve humanity. Babaji had millions of followers. His entourage today included a journalist called Jogi.

Jogi could scarcely believe his eyes. In the past, he had seen Baba plucking Rolex watches from the thin air and giving them to his special guests, people who were very rich and donated a lot of money, but no gifts were ever given to the poor. Jogi believed that plucking watches from the air was a trick, an illusion to fool people.

But after the dead man got up, Jogi was cynical no more. He started attending darshan sessions where he and other followers would come to prayer meetings where Babaji lectured his devotees. At the end of the meetings, everyone would queue to touch Babaji's feet and receive his blessings. At one of the press conferences, Jogi asked, "Babaji, there are reports of young female disciples going missing?"

"No one goes missing in this kingdom of God," he replied.

"Sir, what about checking the cctv cameras?"

He seemed irritated with the suggestion. "No more questions from journalists," he ordered.

Doubts flooded in. "If you are holy, where is your empathy? You are full of ego. EGO stands for Edge God Out. Then how can you claim that you are a man of God?"

A message appeared on Jogi's mobile. "If you don't stop spying on Babaji, you will be killed."

On the way to his newspaper office next morning, Jogi turned into a narrow lane. A group of stray dogs almost jumped on his scooter. He panicked and abruptly accelerated. Hearing a shot, he accelerated further with fright. Relieved to reach his office, he saw another message on his mobile. "Stray dogs saved your life today but you won't be so lucky next time."

His editor advised him to leave the city with his family.

One evening in a different city, he saw a big crowd. Someone was addressing them on the loudspeaker. "I had died, I was floating in the space and the stars with bright lights were coming nearer and nearer to me. Our Babaji promises his devotees that he will meet them after death and lead them to heaven. In my case, Babaji decided to bring me back to life. If you don't believe me, ask the doctors at the hospital who certified my death. I can give you the address of the hospital."

People shouted, "Long live Babaji." His devotees were distributing leaflets. "Babaji is coming to your town. Come and get his blessings on ..."

Jogi recognised the speaker. Yes, he was the man who rose from the dead.

He was surrounded by Baba's security people.

Jogi sneaked near him.

Next day, Jogi's mobile rang. "You left a note in my hand?"

"Yes, I did. I'm Jogi, a journalist."

They met at the back of a restaurant.

The man said to Jogi, "My name is Saxena. I've heard about you, you are brave to ask Baba difficult questions. Baba took my wife and threatened to kill my family, if I reported him to the police."

"How is she?"

"I don't know, but once I accidentally entered Baba's meditation room and there she was, massaging his legs along with other women."

"Did she look at you?"

"Yes, but with no recognition. She had dark circles around her eyes. Her eyes seemed drowsy and droopy."

"Was she drugged?"

"Maybe, I don't know."

"Evil man, this Baba."

"I agree."

"How come you died and Baba was there at the right time to bring you back to life?"

"I don't remember my death but I have heard stories of people being killed to demonstrate miracles," said Saxena. "Baba used to say 'people

do meditation to unite with the bigger soul, namely God. I did meditation to conquer people's souls. I have the power to enter other people's bodies and act supernaturally.' I wonder if he put another soul in my dead body? Sometimes I get thoughts I don't recognise as mine.

"Baba was known to visit open crematoriums where a dead body is put on a pyre with wood and oil and a fire is lit. He would cover his body with hot ash from such fires. Maybe Baba had the power to trap souls liberated from dead bodies and use them for evil purposes," whispered Saxena.

Saxena agreed to help police to collect evidence.

One day, frightened but determined, he entered Baba's meditation room. There was no guard outside. The music wafted out from the room. The room was full of smoke.

"Are they all smoking weed?"

He noticed a cctv camera in the room.

He thought, "Maybe the smoke will hide me from the camera?"

He implanted a tiny surveillance camera in a flower pot hanging from the wall, and quickly left.

Next day, the message came that Baba wanted to see him.

Saxena thought, "I've been caught, my game is over. He'll kill me and my wife." He went to Baba's room, trembling all over.

Baba smiled. "People have forgotten that I am the only person in the world, who can give life to a dead person! You'll have to die again, for me to revive you and breathe life into you. I want to be a living God again."

"Sure, Sir. But first may I request to see my wife?"

"Yes, you can meet her tomorrow."

Next day, he waited for his wife in a room. She walked in, looking drowsy. She had bloodshot eyes. Saxena noticed needle marks on her arms.

"The evil Baba has made my wife a drug zombie," he muttered.

Hugging her, he tied a necklace fitted with a mini camera around her neck.

With the help of transmitted material from the cameras and evidence of missing young daughters of devotees found imprisoned, Baba was jailed for life.

Caroline got up with a puzzled look. "Incredible India," she mumbled.

24

Pinky met the oncologist, who told her, "You'll require radiation treatment every day Monday to Friday for three weeks."

"What is this radiation?"

"It destroys cancer cells, shrinks the size of the tumour to prepare for surgery."

"Any side effects?" asked Pinky.

"Radiation can also damage normal tissue around the cancer area," replied the oncologist, before reciting a long list of side effects.

"So many dangers?" Pinky said, surprised.

"Don't worry," replied the doctor. "Most people don't suffer any harm. Any damage to healthy tissues is lessened by targeting tumour with an accurate dose of radiation. The planning CT scan is done for this purpose. Your treatment will start soon."

Back in the ward, Paul was waiting with fruits and flowers.

He hugged her. "How are you, Aunty?"

"As good as can be. Today I saw a serious looking doctor. He is starting radiotherapy."

"Why serious?" asked Paul.

"Because he's a cancer specialist!"

Paul thought, *She is mentally sharp and clear now. I have to be careful with her. But when she returns to the care home, I'll make sure she is back on her sedatives.*

25

The radiation machine was like a huge umbrella, moving and searching for the black cross on her tummy made by the radiographer. Then it stopped.

Will this burn my tummy? thought Pinky. *How come I don't feel any radiation but it can cause so many side effects?*

The radiographer's voice came from behind the radiation screen. "Stay still, please."

Pinky's mind wandered to her childhood when her mum would shout at her, "Why can't you keep still, you restless little monkey?"

It all started one day in her village primary school.

It was a hot summer day. Little Pinky loved drinking a glass of sugarcane juice. She called it refreshing and blissful. Every lunch break, the vendor would stand outside the school grounds with his old machine on his even older cart. The sugarcane will be inserted into the wheels of the machine. He would rotate the wheels of his machine again and again until nothing was left to crush. Out came the juice, full of lovely taste and energy.

One such lunch break, Pinky and her friend came out of the school grounds. After drinking the sugarcane juice, they sat under a mango tree. Pinky opened her lunch tiffin. Coming from nowhere, a monkey snatched the food, quickly running up the tree. Gone was the aloo paratha (flatbread stuffed with potatoes and spices) and a banana.

Sitting on the tree, the monkey peeled the banana from the bottom, throwing the skin down. "How dare you take my food, throwing the banana peel at me?" Pinky started climbing the tree. Her friend called at her to come down.

"I'm coming to get you."

Looking down towards Pinky, the monkey waited until she was near but then jumped to the adjacent tree.

Now Pinky was trapped on the tree. She could not come down. Her friend ran back to school for help.

The scene was shattered by the radiographer's voice. "Your session is finished."

Back in the ward, Caroline brought her tea and biscuits.

"How are you today, Pinky?"

"I live moment to moment. Even twenty four hours is not guaranteed in cancer. You know that the tumour can spread its poisonous tentacles, but Bobby's memories bring me joy," replied Pinky.

Caroline apologised for that morning, when the trainee nurse struggled to find a site for the IV catheter to administer her intravenous medication. "She says despite so many attempts, you encouraged her."

"I think if we patients don't let trainees learn, where will they gain experience?" said Pinky.

"You're a brave person, Pinky. Despite your pains, you never complain. I hope your cancer is eradicated soon."

26

At last, the final radiotherapy session was over.

"Can you help me to get off the table? I feel weak and tired," said Pinky.

The radiographer helped her. "Don't worry. It is the cumulative effect of radiotherapy. Please sit outside for a while. If you have any problem walking, tell me and I'll arrange a wheelchair to take you to the ward."

Sitting in the waiting room, Pinky looked around. She recognised some of the faces. Tired faces belonging to people who'd been having radiotherapy for sometime. No one was talking to each other.

Maybe painful stories are not for sharing, thought Pinky.

The radiographer came to check on her.

"I'll walk, I feel better," said Pinky.

In the hospital corridor utterly exhausted, Pinky stopped. She could not believe her eyes when she saw Seema.

They hugged. She burst into tears.

Seema asked, "Where have you been?"

"In the care home," replied Pinky.

"I visited your house so many times hoping to see you. I only stopped when the for sale sign went up. I thought you'd gone to India."

"Is my house for sale?" asked Pinky, eyes wide and her hands shaking.

"You don't know?" asked Seema.

"Paul told me I'd return home when the damage is repaired. Was he lying?"

Seema held her hands and they walked to the hospital cafeteria. Sitting together having tea, Seema told Pinky that she was going to take her home.

"I'll look after you. You've lost so much weight. We'll visit our Sikh temple and pray for your good health. All your suffering will be gone."

"You've cheered me up. I already feel better thinking of visiting the gurdwara," said Pinky.

Seema accompanied Pinky back to the ward.

The doctor was planning to discharge her to the care home, but with Pinky's consent, Seema's address was given and the doctor arranged for the district nurse to visit.

On entering Seema's house later that day, tears streamed down Pinky's face. "Ever since Bobby's death, my life's been upside down. All that time, I've felt mentally foggy."

Seema hugged her. She reassured her that everything would be alright now.

That night, they chatted a lot.

Seema was surprised that Pinky remembered so little of events after Bobby's death. "You sent me a message from your mobile not to disturb you so you could grieve in peace."

"I don't recollect sending any such message," replied Pinky. "Why would I? You know any problem in my life, I would run to you."

"That's why I didn't believe it. I came to your house. Even

called you on your mobile from your door. But there was no reply."

Seeing Pinky getting confused, Seema changed the subject. They chatted happily about the good times they'd had together.

27

Next day, Pinky visited her bank with Seema.

The cashier refused to deal with Pinky.

Pinky's voice choked with anger. "I am Pinky Kohli. This is my account. Call the manager."

Sitting in the manager's office, Pinky wanted to know why she was refused access to her own money.

"I'm sorry, but Paul Kohli is the only name who is allowed to access this account."

"Can't you see this account is mine, has been for many years. When my husband died, our joint account became my sole account. This is fraud. Please cancel Paul's name."

"Sorry, I'm unable to do that," replied the manager.

"Please tell me the reason?"

"For legal reasons, I cannot."

"Then you must freeze my account to prevent further fraud."

The manager told Pinky that the account was empty.

Angrily, Pinky shouted, "A fraudster has emptied all my

savings. You let him do it. But when I complain, you stop me. I'll see you in court."

The manager told Pinky, "It is in your interest to take legal advice."

After the shock of the bank, they visited Pinky's house.

Seeing the *for sale* sign, she fell against Seema's chest sobbing. A tidal wave of grief engulfed her. "This house is full of memories of Bobby. What's happening, I can't understand?"

Seema hugged her. "Don't worry, I know someone who will help. A good lawyer. Let's go to his office."

Sitting with the solicitor, Pinky narrated the story since Bobby's death.

Mr Robinson phoned the estate agent selling Pinky's house. "Has the exchange of contracts taken place? I want you to be aware that this is fraud. Paul Kohli is not the owner."

Mr Robinson warned the estate agent not to proceed with the sale and telephoned the land registry, where he learned that Paul Kohli was the legally named owner.

Mr Robinson advised Pinky to report the fraud to the police and land registry property fraud team and added, "Don't worry, I'll find out how Paul managed to empty your savings and transfer your home title deeds to his name. I 'm going to write to the bank, the land registry and the estate agent. When I have enough evidence, I'll file a court case against Paul Kohli."

Pinky left his office in tears.

28

Visiting the ward, Paul was told by the nurse, "Pinky was discharged yesterday."

Driving to the care home, Paul was pleased. *Now the sedatives will work their magic.*

On reaching the care home, surprised that Pinky wasn't there, he phoned the hospital and was told that she'd been discharged to an address he recognised.

Shaking, hands trembling, he called his dad. "Really bad news. Pinky's gone from hospital to Seema's house."

"How come?"

"I don't know, but what if they report the fraud to the police? Should we get out of UK?"

"No, wait. Can you contact the estate agent to speed up the sale?"

"What do I tell the care home?"

"Nothing. After a few days, Pinky might return there. Let's hope for the best," advised Ranjit.

When Paul phoned the estate agent, the agent informed him about the conversation with Pinky's solicitor and that, not wanting to buy a disputed property, the purchaser had pulled out.

Now Paul was very worried. He advised his dad, "We should leave the country quickly."

"No, let's sit tight. Wait and watch."

"Don't forget, Dad, lots of funds were transferred to your name from Pinky's account. You'll be charged too."

29

In the solicitor's office, Mr Robinson was checking all the correspondence received. From Pinky's bank, a letter explained that Pinky's account had been put under management of Mr Paul Kohli as per the power of attorney.

A letter from the psychiatrist Dr Verma stated that he had diagnosed Pinky to be suffering with Alzheimer's disease. According to his mental capacity assessment, he concluded that Pinky Kohli lacked mental capacity to manage her finances and property.

Mr Robinson arranged an independent mental-capacity assessment by a consultant psychiatrist.

The report came back from this psychiatrist with the conclusion as follows:

> Mrs Pinky Kohli does not suffer with Alzheimer's or any form of Dementia. Her cognitive function is not impaired.
>
> I, Mr David Mills, consultant psychiatrist declare that Mrs Pinky Kohli has full mental capacity to manage her finances and property.

Mr Robinson filed a report of fraud with the police against Mr Paul Kohli and his psychiatrist, Mr Verma.

When Pinky read the psychiatrist's report, she was devastated. How could someone whom she had treated as her son do this to her? *My faith teaches me that the light of God resides in every human being.* How would she ever trust anyone again?

30

Seeing Pinky feeling low, Seema thought, *I know how to lift her mood. She used to love kitty parties, playing cards and joking with her friends.*

The kitty party was arranged.

Seema made pakoras with spinach and cauliflower. Pinky declared them, "Delicious, crispy and spiced."

Pinky prepared papdi chaat using crisp fried dough wafers-papri along with boiled chickpeas and potatoes. With tamarind chutney in yogurt, the chaat was ready.

In walked Pinky's friends.

Hugging each of them in turn, she cried, "I thought I'd never see you again."

Sitting to eat, they chatted about good old times while enjoying the pakoras and the chaat.

After that, the card games started.

"Sorry, I'm not playing for money as I have problems accessing my bank account," said Pinky.

Her friends told Pinky, "You are more precious than money. Our memories of you and Bobby are everlasting."

"In fact, my happiest moments are my memories of Bobby," said Pinky.

"With lovely husband memories, you are blessed," her friend Jas told her. "Some months after my husband's death, I was cleaning the house when I found his diary. It read:

Dating Jas, November 72

It is a cold dull day. Meeting Jas is the most beautiful moment of my life. Even after coming home, I cannot forget her lovely smile. I have fallen in love. When I am with Jas, it feels so magical.

December 72

I look forward to meeting Jas. My heart yearns to see her. When I see her, my heart skips a beat with excitement. I have decided that my soulmate will be Jas.

But do you know what the last entry in the diary was?

May 93

Living with Jas is becoming unbearable. For my peace of mind, I need separation. But how do I ask her? She is cold, stupid and stubborn. When she is not at home, I feel happy and contented. When I see her, my heart beats faster not with love but anxiety."

Jas asked Pinky, "Now tell me, how can I have good memories?"

Another friend, Rimi, described a typical day with her ex husband, in which they were arguing over a trivial issue.

"Why don't you go to your favourite library and leave me in peace?" he shouted.

"It's closed," she replied.

"Why?"

"The council's run out of money."

"Thank God the pubs are not dependent on the council."

"Why don't they open a library in the pub?" remarked Rimi.

"Oh no, I go to pub to get away from you," he replied.

"Your failing memory will get better if you read books in your pub, which you visit every day."

"It is you who is causing my memory to fail," he replied.

"Oh no, it is your alcohol. If books were in your pub, you'd be sober reading them. Books are food for thought, a cause of healthy brain. It is the alcohol which poisons your body and brain."

"Go find another library and leave me in peace!" he shouted.

Rimi finished her story and all the ladies laughed.

The main meal arrived: chole-bhature, which is spiced chickpea curry with a soft fluffy fried leavened bread.

"Every time I eat this dish, it reminds me of Punjab," said Seema. "But wait for the dessert, it will remind you of your village vendors, a true street dessert Jalebi."

Bright orange coloured Jalebi is sweet, deep fried made by deep frying a wheat flour batter into circular shapes.

Sitting for masala chai, Seema put on bhangra music.

"For old times' sake, come on Pinky. Let's dance."

Pinky got up reluctantly but she was her old self soon, dancing merrily.

All the ladies joined her.

They left laughing.

"What a party," said Pinky. "Never thought I'd have so much fun."

"Thanks to you, my friend," said Seema lightly. "I'm just glad I have you back."

31

The court case started in the absence of the accused, Mr Paul Kohli, as he had absconded and could not be located.

The other accused, Dr Ajit Varma, was present.

Dr Verma declared that he was a psychiatrist with more than twenty years' experience.

The prosecutor started his questioning.

"On 16th of July 1996, you diagnosed Pinky Kohli with Alzheimer's disease. You declared her mentally incompetent to manage her finances and property. Is this correct?"

"Yes."

"How was your diagnosis done?" asked the prosecutor.

Dr Verma looked at his notes. "Paul, her nephew, told me that Pinky Kohli has hearing problems but she could lipread. After I obtained her permission, he interpreted for her. The risk of dementia in deaf people is significantly higher. The mental assessment including memory tests indicated Alzheimer's."

"Were your dementia screening tests designed for deaf people?"

"Because Pinky could lipread, I screened as I do for non-deaf people," replied Dr Verma.

"Did you offer her a trained interpreter for deaf people?"

"No," replied Dr Verma.

"Did you check if Pinky could read and respond to questions in written English?"

"No," replied Dr Verma.

"Why not?" asked the prosecutor.

"Having to read and respond to questions in written English is not ideal as deaf people do not understand," replied Dr Verma.

"Did you check whether she uses British Sign Language?"

"No."

"Did you order a brain scan?'

"No," replied Dr Verma.

"Were you aware that Pinky's difficulty in hearing was due to not wearing a hearing aid on the day of your appointment?"

"I was not," replied Dr Verma.

The defence lawyer interrupted. "If your patient says that she can lipread, do you believe her?"

Dr Verma replied, "I believe my patient is telling the truth."

The prosecutor continued, "That she could lipread was told to you by Paul Kohli and he is not your patient. He is your patient's relative."

The prosecutor called Dr David Mills, the independent consultant psychiatrist.

"On third of January 97, you examined Pinky Kohli and declared that she is not suffering with Alzheimer's. Your opinion was that she is mentally competent to manage her finances and property."

"Correct," replied Dr Mills.

"In your opinion, why was the original diagnosis incorrect?" asked the prosecutor.

"Pinky Kohli attended then without her hearing aid. If cognitive dementia screening tests for deaf people are not normalised or not designed for deaf people, it can lead to incorrect diagnosis."

"What is your opinion on Pinky not having a brain scan with Dr Verma?"

"Research studies agree that a brain scan used in conjunction with dementia screening tests designed for deaf people allows confident diagnosis of dementia in deaf people," replied Dr Mills.

The defence lawyer took over. He asked Dr Mills, "Can you have dementia with a normal brain scan?"

"Yes," replied Dr Mills

"No more questioning," said the defence lawyer.

The land registry fraud team was called by the prosecutor.

They confirmed that Pinky Kohli's home and two additional properties had been transferred to Mr Paul Kohli's name on the basis of power of attorney.

Finally, the judge ordered Dr Verma's psychiatric report on Pinky Kohli dated 16th July 96 to be sent to dementia specialists working with deaf people for their independent opinion.

Listening to Dr Verma's questioning, Pinky was restless with trembling hands. She started having palpitations and sweating. She was angry at Dr Verma's negligence.

She thought, *you have the power to certify someone Alzheimer's and take away their control in life and you treat that power so casually*.

After a week, the court judge gave his verdict.

"I order the land registry that Mrs Pinky Kohli be

reinstated as the registered owner of her home. Also the two properties named by the land registry fraud team be also re registered under Mrs Pinky Kohli's name."

The Bank was ordered to give access to her accounts and remove Paul Kohli's name. The power of attorney of Pinky Kohli nominating Paul Kohli was declared nul and void.

"I rule that Mr Paul Kohli has committed fraud and sentence him in absentia to seven years' imprisonment."

The judge gave his verdict on Dr Ajit Verma.

"After taking advice from specialists working with deaf people, I rule that Dr Ajit Verma has been negligent in his diagnosis of Alzheimer's in the case of Mrs Pinky Kohli. I am referring him to General Medical Council to investigate him further. I have recommended that he should be suspended from practising until completion of GMC investigations."

With a huge smile, Pinky said to Mr Robinson, "Today, walking in the morning mist, I thought that my brain fog has cleared but will the mist disappear from my life also? Thanks to you for winning the court case, the mist has disappeared."

Hugging Seema, Pinky said, "Without your support ..." But then she burst into tears, tears of gratitude.

Seema hugged her tight.

32

Pinky visited her family doctor and told him of the happenings in her life since Bobby's death, concluding, "A tsunami of problems hit my life and then cancer struck."

"I'm sorry to hear that," replied the doctor. "What's happening about your cancer?"

"I'm on strong painkillers and waiting for surgery."

He studied her computer records. "Pinky, you've missed urgent hospital appointments. Why?"

"I didn't receive any appointments. Perhaps they were sent to the care home?"

"Don't worry, I'll send an urgent email to your surgical consultant with your correct home address and your mobile number."

Within a few days, she got a call.

"Good morning. Are you Mrs Pinky Kohli?"

"Yes."

"I'm from the pre-assessment team at your hospital. Your operation date is Tuesday. I'm here to answer any questions regarding the surgical procedure and anaesthesia. Let's start with some screening questions."

"Sure."

"Are you on medication?"

"Yes. Painkillers, which I take regularly for my tummy pains."

"Your hospital records show that you are on antidepressants?"

"I don't take anymore," replied Pinky.

"Any allergies?"

"No."

After completing her list of questions, she explained, "You will be admitted on Monday. The anaesthetist will check you in the ward. The surgeon will also see you. He'll explain the procedure and risks. He'll ask you to sign a consent form."

Pinky asked about fasting instructions for the general anaesthesia, which were explained to her.

"I wish you good luck from the pre-assessment team. Enjoy the rest of the day."

Pinky spent the rest of the day and the week worrying.

On Monday, Pinky was admitted to the ward.

The anaesthetist visited her. After going through her medical history, he checked her heart and lungs.

Next morning, the nurse took her to the operating theatre.

Looking at the surgical site mark on her tummy, Pinky wondered if the mark was in the right place. She'd heard horror stories where a surgeon had operated on the wrong side of the abdomen. She was worried but frightened of asking the nurses.

In the theatre, all she remembered was sleeping quickly when the anaesthetist injected something into her blood cannula.

With Pinky unconscious, the anaesthetist wanted to pass a

breathing tube through her mouth and down her throat into the lungs. He tried different breathing tubes but none was going into the airway passage.

The anaesthetist's assistant gave him different types of special tubes to try. His hands trembled as he focussed all his attention on placing the tube into the trachea to help with her breathing.

The surgeon was scrubbed and ready to start the surgery.

Seeing beads of sweat on his forehead, he asked the anaesthetist, "What's happening?"

The anaesthetist told the surgeon, "I've failed to intubate. The airway is very difficult. I cannot pass the breathing tube."

The monitoring equipment flashed to indicate oxygen saturation was going down. Pulse rate and blood pressure were getting worst. Pinky's breathing was getting shallow.

In the next door operating theatre, was an experienced senior anaesthetist. He was called and quickly took over and managed to intubate.

With Pinky's breathing settled, oxygen saturation returned to normal. To everyone's relief, all the observations became normal.

The surgeon got the go-ahead for the surgery and the affected part of the bowel was removed. The rest of the procedure was uneventful.

From the recovery room where the anaesthetist checked her chest, heart and observations, Pinky was transferred to the post-operative surgical ward.

In the ward, the surgeon told Pinky, "The cancer has not spread. There were no problems in the surgery. But you gave us a fright during the start of anaesthesia with failed intubation when the breathing tube would not pass into your airway passage. Fortunately, a senior anaesthetist who works with maxillofacial and ENT surgeons and has the expertise of intubating patients with difficult airway, took over. He has advised that you be issued a difficult airway card. You must always carry it with you so that in case of an emergency, the anaesthetist is aware. It can be life-saving."

"That was frightening. Is it common?" asked Pinky.

"No, it is quite rare," replied the surgeon. "But the senior anaesthetist did query if you are taking any other medication not listed in your records which might have aggravated your breathing emergency."

Pinky replied, "I only take what is prescribed to me."

That night, Pinky had severe abdominal pains. The nurse called the doctor, who administered intravenous morphine. "Don't worry, these are post-operative pains." She needed strong painkillers.

After three days, drips and drains came out. She was able to eat.

But when she finally opened her bowels, it was sheer bliss.

She remembered Bobby telling her that after a surgical procedure on his prostate, when he finally managed to pass urine, it was a heavenly experience. She'd laughed at him then.

After Pinky's discharge from the hospital, Seema took her home to care for her.

The ward nurse arranged for the district nurse's house visits to check Pinky's abdomen and wound care.

33

On his walk in a Delhi park each morning, Paul missed his dog in Edinburgh.

One day, after eating in a restaurant, Paul had his leftovers of chicken curry, chapati and rice, packed. He proceeded to the marketplace, where stray dogs congregated. When he saw a little dog salivating and looking unwell, he decided to feed this dog first

Despite his shock when the dog jumped at him and bit his leg, Paul nevertheless ignored the bite and fed the dogs.

After about two weeks, he felt weak and feverish.

Ranjit gave him paracetamol and Paul seemed to be getting better, until one night, Ranjit woke up at hearing a loud bang downstairs.

On coming down, he saw the TV was on the floor and Paul was kicking it again and again. He had red eyes, a foaming mouth, and his hands were shaking.

"Why are you breaking the television? Have you gone crazy?" asked Ranjit.

"It was spying on me. Look at the wires behind, it was planning to strangle me to death with them."

Ranjit sat him down and gave him a glass of water.

Paul took a sip and started gasping for breath. He pushed past his dad and ran upstairs, terror in his eyes.

Ranjit took him to the accident and emergency department of the government hospital. It was difficult to keep him restrained as he was anxious and restless.

At last, after a long wait, he was seen by the doctor.

The doctor asked, "How long has he suffered with mental-health problems?"

"He doesn't. This strange behaviour is recent. He hasn't been going outdoors and looks at everyone suspiciously. He's been sleeping poorly and pacing around the house all night," replied Ranjit.

"What's happened recently?" asked the doctor.

"Nothing."

"Think back. Any events or unusual happenings in his life?" probed the doctor.

"The only incident I can recall is that about three weeks ago, he came home with a cut under his knee. Said he'd been feeding a stray dog, who bit him. He was well after that, even his leg wound healed quickly," replied Ranjit.

The doctor examined him. "I'm afraid the dog bite, hallucinations and the hydrophobia – fear of water – are suggestive of rabies."

Ranjit began to sob. "Paul had strong views against cruelty to animals. He read in the newspaper that a man feeding stray dogs was assaulted by people who didn't want these dogs in their area. They'd chase and beat these dogs with sticks. This made Paul more determined to help the strays," said Ranjit.

Ranjit visited Paul in the hospital twice a day.

The doctor told Ranjit, "I inserted the needle into the

lower part of the spine to remove the cerebrospinal fluid. This is the fluid that surrounds the brain and the spinal cord. Tests on the spinal fluid have revealed that your son is suffering with rabies. When the rabies virus reaches the brain, the chances of coming out alive are very low. I'm afraid rabies is virtually always fatal at this stage."

Tears rolled down Ranjit's cheeks.

Paul lay in the hospital bed, confused and disorientated.

Sitting at his bedside, Ranjit's memories drifted to his conversations with Paul about stray dogs. He remembered saying to him, "Instead of harping all the time about saving stray dogs, why don't you think of helping poor people?"

Paul had replied, "Dogs give unconditional love. I love them."

One day, Paul had been thrilled to read a good-news story about a stray dog.

A man called Avinash decided to adopt a stray dog, despite strong objections from his parents. He named the hound Lucky, because happiness was what Avinash felt when they were together.

Slowly, even his parents took a liking for Lucky.

Once, his parents were away on holiday. Avinash returned home from a friend's party where he had more drinks than usual and collected Lucky from his neighbour's house.

When Avinash took his evening dose of insulin for his diabetes he suddenly felt dizzy. His hands were trembling, he was sweating profusely and weak all over. He slowly walked to the kitchen to get a glass of water. He felt his heart sinking. He was drowsy and fell. He was on the floor, unconscious. Lucky was feeding in the kitchen. He started barking and circling Avinash repeatedly. He was restless and agitated.

Then he jumped out of the kitchen window and ran to the neighbour's house. He was barking and running back and forth. The neighbour came over and was surprised to see Avinash on the floor, not responding. He called an ambulance.

The paramedic checked his blood sugar.

It was desperately low. The medic put a needle in his arm and glucose was given intravenously. He made a full recovery.

The medic said, "It seems, you injected more than your dose of insulin. Your blood sugar was so low that if you hadn't received treatment, you would have died."

Avinash remembered that he had injected insulin twice.

He thanked the doctor. "I'm sorry, I was under the influence of alcohol."

"Thank God you had prompt medical attention," replied the doctor.

"It was my pet, a previous stray dog, who saved my life."

The next day, the local newspaper told his story with the heading, 'Stray dog saves a life'.

ON BEING TOLD ABOUT PAUL'S SERIOUS CONDITION, RANJIT'S neighbour suggested Gurdwara Bangla Sahib near Connaught Place. He said, "Go and pray there. It is a very spiritual place associated with healing. A Sikh historical and holy house of worship."

Despite being an atheist, Ranjit decided to visit early next morning.

It was four a.m. and there were hundreds of devotees in the white marbled gurdwara with stunning gold dome.

Ranjit joined a long orderly queue of devotees.

In front of the holy book, he bowed and prayed, "Forgive me and my son. Have mercy on us. Please save Paul's life."

Coming out, he took karah parshad, a blessed sacred food given to all devotees.

For Paul, he took holy water from the gurdwara along with the parshad.

There was a large pond in the grounds. Its waters were claimed to have healing properties.

Then he returned to the hospital. He prayed at Paul's bedside. "God, please save his life."

Holding his son's hands, he cried for mercy.

Paul had daily injections and was put on an intravenous drip. Slowly, he began responding to treatment. After nine weeks, he had recovered enough to be discharged home.

The doctor said, "I have never seen a case of such advanced rabies being cured. It is a miracle."

Ranjit visited Gurdwara Bangla Sahib to thank the Almighty.

At home, Ranjit requested Paul never to feed stray dogs.

Paul thought, *The poor dog gave me rabies. It wasn't his fault. He was ill himself. He's probably dead by now. Why blame all the stray dogs?*

34

When Paul had fully recovered, Ranjit organised a trip to old Delhi to cheer him up. In the auto rickshaw, they travelled to the Red Fort.

Entering the fort, they were surprised how huge the walls stood. The fortifications were made from red sandstone and had white marble embellishments.

The guide told the tourists, "Old Delhi was founded as a walled city in 1648 by the Mughal emperor, Shah Jahan. It was the capital of the Mughal empire. Shah Jahan loved art and architecture. During his reign, the Red Fort and massive grand Jama Masjid were built. Both are masterpieces of Mughal architecture. An enduring symbol of Mughal grandeur and craftsmanship, the Red Fort served as the main residence of the emperor. It's a UNESCO World Heritage Site. Outside the fort is an area called Chadni chowk."

He gave a description of Chadni chowk during the Mughal era. "The magnificent mansions with wide tree-lined boulevards, marketplaces and squares teemed with life and commerce. The old Delhi history reflected the fusion of various cultures and traditions. It saw the blending of Persian, Indian and central Asian influences resulting in a rich tapestry of art, architecture, cuisine and language that continues to be celebrated today."

One of the tourists asked, "What happened to the reign of this emperor?"

"After Shah Jahan recovered from an illness in 1658, his son Aurangzeb imprisoned him in the fort of Agra. Aurangzeb declared himself emperor. Shah Jahan lived the last decade of his life as his son's prisoner," the guide replied.

Another tourist asked, "Why was he imprisoned by his son?"

"Greed and power," replied the guide. "After his death, Shah Jahan was laid to rest next to his wife, Mumtaz, in the Taj Mahal. In memory of Mumtaz, Shah Jahan had commissioned the Taj Mahal in 1631 after her death. It was a great love story, famous all over the world. But all he got from his son was hatred and death."

"What a history of love and hatred," whispered a tourist.

Paul and Ranjit came outside the gate to Chadni chowk. Paul said, "What we see now is poles apart from the Chadni chowk of Mughal era."

Within the narrow lanes were cycle rickshaws, wooden carts, vendors, scooters and cars.

Dodging puddles, rickshaws and cows, they reached a tiny alley, all the stalls cooking Parathas, the popular Indian flatbread with stuffing. The alley was even called, "Paratha wali gali," meaning paratha street.

They couldn't decide which stall to eat from.

Ranjit said, "In India, if a food stall has the most people waiting outside, then it is probably good."

So, they joined the biggest queue.

The cook filled the dough with everything from potatoes

to paneer, from cashews to rabri (a thick sweetened milk dessert). The parathas were deep fried in front of the customers and served hot with assorted chutneys and vegetables. Paul had one paneer (cottage cheese) and one cauliflower paratha, while Ranjit had mint and lemon paratha. Both drank lassi (thick sweetened buttermilk). Ranjit loved the parathas but Paul found them too spicy and heavy.

Walking through the bustling markets, shops selling textiles, spices, jewellery and a traditional Indian bazaar, they found business being done at frantic pace with deliveries of goods carried on people's heads, carts and bicycle rickshaws.

Paul noticed that the lines on the road were merely decorative, for no one followed the rules. He also observed that one-way streets were not really one-way streets in Chadni chowk.

Escaping the chaos, the noise and constant car horns, they entered Gurdwara Sis Ganj Sahib. The martyrdom site of the ninth Sikh guru, Guru Tegh Bahadur, it was an oasis of tranquility. He was beheaded in 1675 by the then Mughal emperor, Aurangzeb.

The Guru protected the faith and honour of the persecuted and the downtrodden. He gave his supreme sacrifice protecting those whose religion was being forcibly converted. He is still remembered as the Hind Di Chadar (Shield of India).

Sitting in the serene surroundings, tears gathered at the corner of Paul's eyes. He meditated and reflected, "Pinky trusted me. She gave me love as a son and in return I gave her hatred with my greed and cheated her."

He asked for forgiveness.

Ranjit was surprised to see Paul praying. Coming out of the gurdwara, Ranjit asked, "I thought you didn't believe in God?"

Paul replied, "Sitting inside, something strange welled up in my mind. A voice told me that if you want peace and happiness in your life, then show love and kindness to all. Hatred will only bring misery to your life."

He asked his dad if this was a warning from God after what they'd done to Pinky.

Ranjit quickly changed the subject. "What a history lesson from the Mughal emperor, who built the world famous Taj Mahal."

"As well as the history of beheading of our Sikh guru by the son of this Mughal emperor. Dad, please answer my question about our deceit with Pinky."

Ranjit sat on the pavement at the side of the road and began to sob uncontrollably.

"I am a sinner. I have ruined your life. With greed and love for money, I became an evil man. My grandfather taught me kindness and charity for the needy, but I hated this world. I never told you but I prayed at the Gurdwara Bangla Sahib and you got cured from rabies. Your hospital consultant called your cure a miracle."

With tears running down his cheeks, Paul thanked his dad for his prayers. "I want to visit Gurdwara Bangla Sahib so I can offer my prayers in gratitude."

"We'll visit together, my son."

35

Next morning, Paul's mobile rang. A voice he didn't recognise asked, "Is this Paul Kohli?"

"Yes, speaking."

"We need your address," the stranger said.

Cautiously, Paul asked, "Who are you?"

"Police," came the answer, swiftly followed by, "We know you're in India."

"Why do you need my address?" Paul tried not to sound as worried as he now began to feel.

"You have been found guilty of criminal fraud in the British court and sentenced to seven years' imprisonment in absentia."

"Sorry for interrupting, sir. I think you have mistaken me for someone else."

The answer from the caller came back, like a ball throw by a fast bowler. "Have no doubt, Paul, we will find you and you will be arrested."

Paul broke out in a sweat and put the phone down. He called his dad and told him briefly what had just transpired. He began to cry.

"No time to cry. We must leave this place and find somewhere safe to hide."

"Look where your revenge for Bobby has taken us, Dad. How I wish I'd never listened to you."

Both of them were shocked and fearful of being handcuffed and put in an Indian jail before being transferred to a British jail.

A friend agreed to move them to his house. He advised them to go to Nepal. "You'll be safe there."

They booked a flight from Delhi to Kathmandu, Nepal.

It was August 1997, monsoon season.

The heatwave had been replaced by torrential rains, thunder and blinding flashes of lightning. The parched earth was now flooded with the smell of wet earth.

The taxi arrived to take them to the airport. The driver warned that many roads were flooded so he would have to take a longer route.

On the way, he stopped at the petrol station.

"Can you please pay for the fuel?" asked the taxi driver.

Ranjit paid but was annoyed. "Why can't you fill the tank before picking a customer?"

But then Ranjit remembered a friend telling him that it was often done purposely. When a customer reaches the airport, he is so stressed that he forgets he has paid for the fuel.

The traffic was slow, cars trying to dodge the huge potholes.

Finally arriving at Delhi airport, Ranjit was relieved.

The taxi driver looked at his meter. "Two thousand seven hundred rupees plus five hundred for your luggage." Ranjit paid him less, deducting for the fuel he had already paid. The driver wasn't happy.

Grabbing the trolley, they ran to the check in counter where there was a long queue.

After check-in, Paul nervously approached the immigration desk. The immigration officer looked at his passport and at the computer screen. He looked at Paul and again at his computer screen. He now had a suspicious look on his face. He raised his eyebrows and said, "You have overstayed in India and cannot leave the country until you acquire an exit permit visa from the Foreigners Regional Registration office in Delhi."

Paul's heart sank. Next in queue was Ranjit. Seeing Paul walking back, Ranjit quickly joined him.

On the way back to his friend's house in a taxi, he constantly looked over his shoulder in case the police were following. "What if I'm arrested in the FRRO office?"

Ranjit had no answer.

Next morning, when they arrived at the FRRO, the office was full of distressed foreigners.

A young American lady told Paul, "I achieved calmness and tranquility in an Indian yoga centre, which was shattered when I wasn't allowed to board my flight because my Indian visa had expired just one day before. When I went back to my hotel, they refused me a room. I've been coming to this office daily and providing various documents, which they scrutinise thoroughly, and then ask for more information."

Frightened, Paul left the office without applying for the exit visa. Ranjit followed him.

They decided to take the risk and leave India via the Nepal border. The plan was to travel by taxi to Kathmandu, capital city of Nepal.

They took the train to the Indian city of Gorakhpur, 72 miles from the Nepal Sunauli border, and then a taxi, arriving at the border in the evening.

It looked like a crowded marketplace. Indians and Nepalese

do not need a visa to enter each other's country but all vehicles are checked thoroughly by the police. As he and Paul slowly walked to the small immigration office, Ranjit's hands were sweaty and trembling. His mind raced. He noticed with relief that there were no computers in the office, so their refusal at Delhi airport might not become apparent.

Ranjit, looking tense and nervous, showed his British passport to the young immigration officer, who began his many questions with asking the purpose of their visit to Nepal.

"To have a holiday."

"Why didn't you fly from Delhi to Kathmandu?"

"I wanted to see the beauty of Nepal by road."

"Where are you travelling tonight?"

"To Kathmandu," replied Ranjit.

"Why are you travelling so late at night?" said the officer, a suspicious look on his face. "Take a seat. I'll keep your passport until we make a decision."

"How long will that take?" asked Ranjit.

"The office closes at 8pm. If my officer doesn't return by then, you'll need to come back tomorrow morning."

Ranjit put fifty pounds in an envelope and gave it to him. "This is for you, sir."

"OK, I am stamping your passport, have a safe journey," said the officer with a smile.

The mountain roads were narrow, steep and zig-zagging with deep blind ends. In the dark night and heavy rain, visibility was poor.

The taxi driver said, "You regularly see buses and cars that have fallen off these roads, into the ravines below. These are dangerous roads."

Ranjit asked the driver, "Should we stop?"

"No, don't worry, I'll drive cautiously," chuckled the driver.

"Please stop whenever you get sleepy," advised Ranjit.

"Yes, sir."

Ranjit made sure he stopped at tea stalls for regular breaks.

They reached Kathmandu in the early hours of the morning and found a hotel.

But Paul couldn't sleep.

Seeing Paul restless, Ranjit asked, "Are you OK?"

"I have this recurrent dream of being chased by elephants. I know dreams aren't true, but..."

"No, your dream is true. You are being chased by the British police," chuckled Ranjit.

"I have drowned in your tsunami of greed but you are insensitive to my suffering."

"I'm sorry. Had I known it would lead to this..." Ranjit burst into tears. "I think of it last thing every night, first thing every morning and all day. Life is not worth living is my recurrent thought. Sometimes I hear a voice telling me to take my life."

Paul hugged him. "I need you, Dad. Please never think of taking your life."

Next morning, the rain stopped. Bazaars and streets were crowded, noisy and chaotic. Everywhere loud hawkers, loud music and loud honking.

Paul thought, "I need the peace and calm of Edinburgh."

But inside the Buddhist shrine was peaceful.

After shopping, they went back to the hotel through narrow backstreets where they noticed that food and fresh fruit was cheaper.

They felt safer in the backstreets, too.

36

Running short of money, Paul applied for a job as an English teacher. Being unsuccessful in Kathmandu, he applied in countryside schools. Most paid a paltry amount, but one school funded by an American organisation offered better wages and free accommodation. It was a primary village school in the foothills of the Himalayas.

He attended for an interview and found it was a steep climb up to the stone school building.

Being successful in getting the job, he was shown his accommodation, a stone-walled house on the hill.

Paul returned to Kathmandu via a long tiring bus journey on muddy roads.

He told Ranjit, "It is a beautiful place. No one will find us there."

That night, he slept peacefully.

After two days, they travelled to the village school. Ranjit liked their house on the hill with majestic views.

In the morning, the mountain mist was magical and mystical.

School did not start before 10am because many children walked an hour or more on the mountain paths to get there. On arrival, the children assembled in front of the school. There was not enough flat space so children were divided into two groups. They attended classes with a blackboard and sat on old wooden benches.

Roll call was taken from the class register.

"Good morning, sir," replied each student.

Paul introduced himself.

He found his students were filled with affection and respect.

It was a pleasure to teach them. The children's eyes were shining with excitement.

On his second day, the students welcomed him with pickled plums, fruits and vegetables grown on their farms.

Paul was touched.

He asked a student, "What time do you get up to come to school?"

"When my farm cocks crow in the morning," the boy replied. "It's a long walk to the school."

The first weekend, Paul took his dad around the area.

The village had bamboo huts as well as some houses with stone walls and thatched tin roofs. Tibetan prayer flags flew all over. The village open spaces were lush with bright green vegetables. Terraced along mountainsides using all possible space from the rugged terrain, were paddy fields where farmers worked using simple tools.

Ranjit watched an old woman climbing up steep terraces carrying a basket. It seemed the whole family were involved in farming, even grandparents.

Ranjit enquired of a farmer, "Even the elderly work in the farm? What do they carry on their backs?"

He replied, "The elderly have to work as lots of young people migrate to Kathmandu."

He explained that the carrying basket made from bamboo, handwoven in a v-shape was called a doko. It was strapped on their head and shoulders and placed on the back.

Outside the village, were enthralling majestic waterfalls. On the way back, they saw monsoon clouds playing hide and seek with the mountain peaks.

Paul said, "It is a mystical sight."

Ranjit agreed.

On Monday, a teacher in his school gave him a gift of traditional Nepalese costume. Her name was Jasmine. She taught Nepali language. A nineteen year old, five feet three inches tall, fair skinned with a baby face, she wore her curly black hair in a tidy ponytail.

As time went on, Paul found her to be a bubbly, cheerful person.

Her father was a farmer.

Seeing Jasmine talk in Nepali language, Paul commented, "It is quite similar to Hindi, the national language of India."

"Yes but with some differences," replied Jasmine.

"Even the Nepali greeting *Namaste* is Hindi," Paul added.

They enjoyed each other's company, chatting and laughing together.

She brought him home-cooked food. Paul's favourite was rice, lentil soup and vegetable curry. She called them bhaat, daal and tarkari.

One day, Jasmine brought momos.

Paul asked, "What are these?"

"Our traditional cuisine in Nepal."

"How are they made?"

"I made the outer covering with a white flour and water dough. The filling inside is minced meat, potatoes and leek. For vegetarians, I make the filling with veggies and paneer, the cottage cheese."

"What are these two sauces?" asked Paul.

"This is aachar, a spicy tomato-based dipping sauce. The other one is a chutney. I make it from mint and coriander," replied Jasmine. "No more questions, just eat!"

"So tasty, full of flavours. I love it."

"I will bring your love every day," replied Jasmine.

One day, Paul asked if they could meet outside the school.

She replied, "Such meetings are disapproved of in our village community, but let's meet at a lonely riverside place,"

Sitting on the bank of a crystal clear, roaring river flowing straight down the snow-filled Himalayas with rapid speed and crashing waves, Paul found it exhilarating.

He was soon joined by Jasmine.

Sitting on the bank holding hands, Jasmine anxiously looked over her shoulder each time she heard a sound.

"Why so nervous? Don't you trust me?" asked Paul.

"I trust you, but if my parents come to know that I am meeting you, they will be very annoyed. Meeting before marriage is frowned upon here."

Paul looked into her flashing beautiful big brown eyes. "You are the most precious thing in my life. I love you. I want to marry you."

"I love you but I'm frightened. My parents believe only in traditional arranged marriages. They are convinced that arranged marriages are made in heaven so are always successful."

Jasmine told him a true story of an arranged marriage, narrated to her by her grandfather.

It was a wedding night.

The bridegroom Daksh entered the bedroom and saw his wife, Bhagwati, still decked in jewellery with her bridal veil, sitting on the bed. He quickly got into the bed.

Lifting her veil, his face turned from joy to anger. "No, you are not the woman I agreed to marry."

She whispered, *"It was me you saw, when you came to my house with your parents. I brought the tray of tea, ladoos and gulab jamun, as is the tradition in arranged marriages. Don't you remember, my mother announced that I had made the sweets and I was a good cook?"*

"But I said yes to the young woman sitting on the settee opposite to me with your parents," he said.

"That was my younger sister."

He got up and went to his parents' bedroom.

He shouted at his father, "I have been deceived. I have been married to the wrong sister."

His father said, "Son, it's been a long day of religious rituals and celebrations. You are tired. You will be alright tomorrow."

"No, she is not alright. She is squint-eyed. She is fat. Her sister was petite, had light coloured skin and long, fair hair. I still remember her radiant smile."

"Son, you had better forget the sister and her radiant smile. Your wife is Bhagwati. You did the pheras around the sacred fire with the priest chanting from the religious texts. In our religion, marriage is a sacred union between two souls, united as one. Once marriage rites are completed, it is a sin to think of another woman."

"There will be no union between our bodies and souls in this marriage," shouted Daksh.

He stormed out of his father's room, banging the door in anger.

In his bedroom, he put a mattress on the floor.

She pleaded with him not to sleep on the floor but he refused.

As he lay down on the floor, she said, "You sleep on the bed, I'll sleep on the floor."

"No."

She gave him the pillows and said, "Good night."

He replied, "This is the worst night of my life."

Bhagwati lay in the bed, crying.

She had studied up to secondary school in her village school. She was a good cook. She was a kind, caring person but today, her husband did not want to know her.

Next day, the mother had a talk with Daksh. "Your name means precious. We did not expect this from you. Your wife cried all night. Try to understand her. When we saw her in her house, she had a broad smile..."

"Yes and a belly to match," retorted Daksh.

"The beauty of a woman is reflected in her soul. Your father never saw my face until after marriage. We adore each other. You are the proof of our marriage."

"Sorry, you won't get proof of our marriage. I do not love Bhagwati."

"Love will come with time and grow with passing years," said his mother. "In our culture, marriage is for life. Do not ever think of leaving her."

Daksh bought a single bed, to sleep separately. Bhagwati was horrified. She felt sad and guilty and thought of returning to her parents' home, but worries about her family honour prevented it.

One day, Daksh developed a high fever. He was diagnosed with typhoid fever. The fever persisted for many weeks. He lost his appetite and was weak and exhausted. Bhagwati looked after him day and night with love and affection. She fed him like a mother feeding a child. As he was dehydrated, she made sure that he drank fluids regularly.

He told her, "You know typhoid is an infectious disease? Please be careful."

She replied, "I am your wife. It is my duty to share your suffering. Your health is more important to me."

It took him more than two months to recover.

One day, he looked in her squinting eyes and said, "Please forgive me. You are the most beautiful person. I love you."

The single bed was removed from the bedroom.

When his mother saw the change in Daksh, she said, "I did not know that an infectious disease could lead to an infectious love."

Paul laughed. "What a lovely story."

Jasmine felt relaxed now.

"Paul, tell me about yourself?"

"I am five feet eight inches, muscular. I have a darkish complexion..."

"Tell me about your childhood, education, family...

"I was born in Edinburgh, Scotland. At present, I am taking a gap year from my university studies in economics."

"Why is your father with you? Most gap students who come to Nepal, come alone."

"First let me tell you about my childhood. When I was a child, we went to visit India. My recollections are as told to me by my father."

"Who were you talking to at the door for an hour?" asked my dad.

"She is my friend. She had no time to come in so we chatted," replied my mother

"One hour at the door!"

"Yes, she is a busy woman."

Paul continued, "But this busy friend came next day and took my mother out in her car. That was the last time I saw my mother. It was a fatal car accident."

"How sad. I am so sorry," said Jasmine.

"My father brought me up. He worried about me going to Nepal. I agreed to let him come with me."

Jasmine said, "I have an idea, if you and your dad agree. For arranged marriages, the boy's dad approaches the girl's father to ask his permission for marriage. Perhaps your father can approach my dad?"

"I will ask him to," replied Paul. "Now, tell me about you?"

"I was born in this village. I attended the village primary school and did my secondary schooling in the nearby town. After passing my exams, I was lucky to get a job in my village school. I love it here. I used to come to this riverbank with my friends and watch the rafters."

"Why are there none today?"

"In monsoons, it is very dangerous because of flooded river and swift currents."

Jasmine with a broad smile on her face described her rafting experience. "I cruised down from magnificent heights, the river hurtling down through the foothills of the Himalayas with beautiful views of forested canyons. Rafting is a thrilling experience. I would love to do it with you. You will cherish the memory all your life."

"We'll do it together."

They walked together holding hands. Jasmine's fear and anxiety had evaporated.

37

Back home, Paul told his dad about Jasmine and her suggestion.

"Did you tell her you are being chased by British police? Or forget it, you do know why she wants to marry you?"

"Why's that?"

"For your British citizenship."

"You're talking nonsense. We love each other. She is a very decent girl, very honest. Her family are not frauds like us."

Next day, Ranjit went to the village.

A boy asked him, "You are our teacher Paul sir's father?"

"Yes," replied Ranjit.

The boy's father invited him in. "It is my daughter's wedding. Please, join us."

Inside, the bride was wearing an embroidered, vibrant red sari decked in jewellery, with the groom in Nepali attire. They greeted him namaste, with folded hands.

Ranjit congratulated them and asked the groom about his outfit.

"It is traditional Nepali outfit called daura suruwal, consisting of an embroidered silk knee-length shirt, a loose fitting trouser and a waistcoat."

Buddhist monks started performing sacred rituals and chanting prayers to bless the couple. Afterwards, there was exchange of fresh flowers garland between bride and groom.

Ranjit found the custom of tying the wedding knot interesting. During this ritual, the couple's hands are bound together with a sacred thread, symbolising their eternal bond.

Ranjit enjoyed the grand wedding feast. He made friends with the bride's father, who taught him about Nepal's marriage customs.

Ranjit found some aspects quite similar to in India, such as marriage is a bonding between the families of bride and groom. The selection of an auspicious wedding date by astrological calculations on the alignment of stars and planets is also followed by many in India.

Ranjit had gone to the village to see Jasmine's father but spent the day celebrating another marriage. He returned home happy.

38

Pinky's life was slowly returning to normal.

Her friends organised a day trip to York, a beautiful historic city only forty miles from Bradford.

Reaching York in the minibus, they joined a long queue of school children at the Viking centre near the city centre.

The costumed Viking staff were entertaining the children.

One staff member carrying an axe was asking questions. "Where did Vikings come from?"

Children raised their hands and shouted, "Denmark, Sweden, Norway."

"What does the word *Viking* mean?"

Children shouted, "Warrior."

"Wrong. Do the teachers know?"

The teachers looked at each other. No-one replied.

"OK, I will tell you the answer. It means a raider."

One boy asked, "Can I have your axe?"

"No," replied the staff member.

The centre opened its doors. After all the children had gone in, Pinky and her friends were allowed to enter.

The guide announced, "Welcome to JORVIK. You are on the actual site of the archaeological dig. The excavation uncovered astonishing evidence of the lives of people who lived in Jorvik (the old name for York) over 1000 years ago, during the city's Viking period."

Pinky was nervous walking on the glass floor. The staff reassured her that it was safe. Under it was a replica of part of the excavation, the remains of two houses.

The staff explained that houses were made from oak planks. They would have had a dug-out cellar and a turf roof.

Visitors were then taken in small carriages showing life-like mannequins and dioramas depicting Viking life in York. Among the interesting archaeological finds were iron keys, door locks, horseshoes, coin die used for striking silver pennies, bird bones, a flute, a sock, leather shoes, glass beads, iron pans and tools. Also notable were pottery vessels, wooden cooking utensils such as spoons and spatulas, bowls and cups with traces of painted decoration, a wooden shovel, spades, knives, double-ended iron spoons, needles and nails and bone ice skates.

The guide said, "Bone evidence suggests that dogs during the Viking period were as big as wolves."

He showed a Viking comb. "These were made from antlers and decorated beautifully."

Seema asked, "Wasn't it cruel to remove the deer antler for making a comb?"

"Deers shed their antlers once a year. They fall off every spring," replied the guide.

He then showed a gaming board. It looked like a chessboard. "This is an oak table game board. The playing pieces were made from antler bone and stones."

Leaving the Viking centre, Pinky said to her friends, "Wasn't it astonishing to get an insight into the lives of Vikings who lived in York more than 1000 years ago. The craftsmen then were quite clever."

Next, they visited the Shambles in York city centre. It is the best preserved medieval shopping street in the world, with its cobbled street and overhanging buildings dating back to the late fourteenth and fifteenth century. It was mentioned in the Doomsday Book of William the Conqueror in 1086.

The ladies took lots of selfies in the Shambles.

"Why do the buildings look bent and protruding?" asked one of the friends.

"When you are so old, your spine will also be bent," replied Pinky.

They all laughed.

Then they walked to the York Minster.

The guide welcomed them. "This is the biggest cathedral in northern Europe. It was founded in 627 AD, which is 1397 years ago. It is the seat of Archbishop of York."

It was indeed big, splashed with stained glass and graced with soaring ceilings.

The guide explained the brilliant gothic architecture.

"What a magnificent cathedral," Pinky exclaimed.

At the end of the tour, the guide showed them a statue inside the York Minster with two right feet. "When the sculptor had completed the right foot, he asked his apprentice to do the left foot but copy how he did the right foot. The apprentice copied exactly for the left foot!"

Back in the minibus, Pinky thought of Bobby and the traumatic events after his death.

"I wish Bobby had been with me in York today."

Her faith gave her strength. She had forgiven Paul. She believed life cannot move on without forgiveness.

39

Ranjit reluctantly visited Jasmine's father.

Entering the gate, there was a long path leading to the front door with a lovely garden on both sides of the path. Ranjit was attracted to the purple flowers. They were full of fragrance. The garden was colourful with mini sunflowers, marigold and yellow oleander flowers.

Opening the door was a middle-aged muscular man.

"Sorry to disturb you. I'm Paul's dad."

"Who's Paul?'

"My son is a teacher at the village primary school," replied Ranjit.

"Sure. Please come in. I am Aatish."

He introduced his wife, Tara.

Sitting down, Ranjit struggled to express the reason for his visit. He was relieved when Tara brought tea and snacks. Serving them, she sat down next to her husband on the sofa.

"You have a beautiful house. It is different from the other village houses."

Aatish was pleased. "Thank you for your kind words. This

is a brick-built house. I will show you the lavish woodcarvings on the windows after we finish our tea. Most of our village houses are made with big stones found in the river bank. Our farm workers live in mud houses, made out of dirt dug up from the same plot of ground where the house is built. The old village houses are traditional bamboo houses."

Ranjit took a deep breath. "Paul and I live in England. My son is in Nepal for his gap year from his university studies. I accompanied him here. He very much likes your daughter, Jasmine. With your permission, he wants to marry her."

There was silence in the room.

Aatish finally spoke. "If my daughter leaves for England, I will be devastated. I lost her once. I don't want to lose her again."

"I am sorry to hear that but how did you lose her?"

Aatish narrated the story.

Walking towards the riverbank were hundreds of saffron-clad sadhus, some naked with ash-smeared bodies. As they took a dip in the water, they chanted, "Har Har Gange" (Mother Ganges).

Also at the river bank was little Jasmine, two years old, with her father Aatish and her mother, Tara. They were attending the world's largest congregation of religious pilgrims, the Kumbh Mela of India.

Where the sacred Ganga and Yamuna rivers merged, millions took a dip in the holy water to purify their souls.

Wearing a marigold garland around her neck, Jasmine lit clay lamps and floated them along the Ganges.

Yesterday, she had been so excited to see elephants, horses and camels with drummers and bands in a colourful procession.

Today they all came at dawn but at sunrise, the riverbank was getting too crowded. Aatish picked up Jasmine. There was commotion, people in front were running backwards. Aatish couldn't understand what was happening. He fell backwards and when he opened his eyes, the early morning sun stung his eyes. He blinked and looked sideways. There, he saw Tara weeping and a crowd around her.

"What happened?" he asked.

"You fell and hit your head. You were unconscious and I couldn't find Jasmine," replied Tara.

The volunteers took them to the lost and found camp, where the government official reassured them. "Don't worry. We have lots of volunteers and police on duty. We find most of the children quickly. Pilgrims, when they see crying children alone, bring them to our centres. Give me your name, addresses and contact details, the details of the child, name, description, a photo if you have one. We have thousands of loudspeakers announcing the names and description of missing persons on our public address system every hour. All our centres share the details of missing people."

They squatted on the ground outside the lost camp. More people joined them. All had registered their missing relatives in the centre. The midday sun was getting stronger. The atmosphere was fraught with tension. Anxious hours had been spent worrying, but Tara could take no more. She sobbed uncontrollably and mumbled, "What if our little Jasmine has been abducted by a gang?"

A woman sitting nearby let out a shrill cry when she saw her missing husband. Both in their eighties, the couple had been married for more than six decades but had been separated that morning. She ran towards him and her relieved husband hugged her.

The official came out of the camp with a list. Everyone stood up.

Aatish's heart was racing. He held his shaking hands tightly.

The list was of missing people who'd been found at other centres. Jasmine's name did not feature on the list.

It was getting dark. The centre closed for the night.

They were staying in a massive tented city erected by the state government and slowly walked back to their camp. All night, they could hear each other's breathing as neither of them could sleep.

They both drifted through their memories.

Aatish aged twenty-five years, well built, 5'10" with dark complexion. He had dropped out of his village school. One day, in his class under the old banyan tree, he was asked by the teacher, "You are looking away while I am teaching, are you not interested?"

"No."

The teacher made him sit with arms crossed holding his ears while kneeling on his bench.

His classmates laughed at him. He felt so humiliated that he refused to return to school. He told his father, "I hate studying. I hate the teacher. I hate my school."

His father, a rich Nepali farmer, taught him the business of farming and how to make the labourers work even harder.

But Aatish was more interested in helping the poor farm labourers. He spent money improving their houses, which leaked every monsoon.

His marriage to Tara was an arranged one. She came from a neighbouring village in Nepal.

She was twenty-two years old, 5'3", a petite girl with a fair complexion. She completed her secondary school and did well in her studies.

After more than five years of trying for a child, they had Jasmine. The family called her a gift from God.

Tara would say, "Jasmine has my light brown eyes and hair. Like me, when she smiles she has a cute dimple on her cheek."

To protect her from any evil eye, Tara put a black dot on Jasmine's cheek.

Tara was shaken from her thoughts by the sound of heavy footsteps and the weight of a hand on her shoulder. It was early morning.

The footsteps were pilgrims walking outside and the hand belonged to Aatish.

Aatish told Tara, "Let's go to the same site at the riverbank. Jasmine might appear miraculously with the mercy of God. On the way, we will pray at the temple." They quickly got ready and joined the pilgrims.

They looked all over the riverbank but there was no trace of Jasmine.

Returning to the lost and found centre, they sat huddled with hundreds of other people, who had also been separated from their friends and family. All looked exhausted and anxious, like them.

When the office opened, Aatish and Tara approached the official.

He said, "I have sent Jasmine's photograph to all police stations and railway stations. Our state border police is on alert and looking for your child."

Tara asked, "Do you suspect Jasmine has been kidnapped?"

"No, no, I am being cautious. All our loudspeakers are constantly blaring out Jasmine's name and description. I am hoping that one of our volunteers will soon bring your child to one of our centres."

Aatish and Tara sat down, outside in the sun.

A man in his fifties came to the centre looking for his father.

The official asked him, "Did you lose him today?"

"No no, I lost him when I was a child. My father visited here on Kumbh Mela and decided to become a sadhu. He left his family and all worldly belongings. To find him, I come every twelve years, when the Khumbh Mela is held here. I was just hoping that this Kumbh, I would find him."

The official replied, "The new sadhus find a guru and live in the Himalayas. They do visit Kumbh Melas but he would be unlikely to get in contact with you as he has already sacrificed his family attachment. A sadhu's life is meditation and prayers. They have no attachment to their bodies, even. They spend all their life focussing their minds in search of God."

"What about my sacrifice, growing up without a father?"

"OK, give me his details and I'll broadcast them on the public-address system."

It was approaching evening. The official came out with a list of found people. Again, no mention of Jasmine.

Whenever they saw someone with a child approaching the tent, they would nervously stand up, hoping the child was Jasmine.

Aatish and Tara were overwhelmed with sadness and helplessness. Every day, sitting outside the lost and found tent, they were losing hope of finding their child. The government official had passed their case to the police. Their dream pilgrimage had turned into their worst nightmare.

The Kumbh was coming to an end. The workers were busy dismantling the tented city. The police promised to contact them as soon as Jasmine's whereabouts was known. They returned to Nepal with heavy hearts.

The whole village was sad. Hindu and Buddhist prayers were performed.

"I cannot breathe, I am dying," said Tara one night.

Aatish quickly got up. "What happened?"

"I don't know. But I'm OK now."

When the episode reoccurred, Aatish took her to the clinic.

The doctor checked her and said, "These are panic attacks, probably related to Jasmine's disappearance."

Aatish whispered to the doctor, "I get thoughts of jumping from the top of my house."

"What other thoughts come in your mind?" asked the doctor.

"If I had not fallen to the ground, my daughter would not have gone missing. I don't deserve to live."

Tara was shocked. She told the doctor, "He doesn't eat and sleep well. When I ask him why, he keeps quiet."

The doctor said, "Aatish is suffering with depression. I am prescribing medication. I will arrange for him to see a psychiatrist, practising in the nearby town."

Tara told Aatish, "It wasn't your fault. It was an accident due to people falling on you."

The doctor encouraged them to talk about Jasmine.

The family elders advised Aatish and Tara to have a baby.

Three years passed without any news of Jasmine.

Aatish's depression had improved. He did not have any further suicidal thoughts.

They tried to have a baby but were unsuccessful.

One night, Aatish got up to find Tara crying. He held her hands and said, "I know you miss Jasmine like me, all the time. Maybe a child in the family would help. What if we adopt a girl, five years old as Jasmine would be now?"

She reluctantly agreed but wanted to adopt in India, where Jasmine was lost.

They went to Delhi and registered to adopt a five-year-old girl.

After about six months, the adoption office called them.

They said, "We have registered today for adoption, a five-and-a half-year-old girl. Her parents died in a car accident. Her uncle, Mr Mishra, brought her to the adoption centre."

Next day, Aatish and Tara arrived in Delhi. At the adoption centre, they waited anxiously. A bald man in his seventies, who they assumed to be Mr Mishra, walked in with a girl.

Tara could not believe her eyes. Amazed, she screamed, "you are my Jasmine."

With tears in her eyes, she hugged the child tightly.

She quickly pulled up child's sleeve.

On her right forearm, there was the religious symbol Om and underneath was written in Hindi, Jasmine.

Hugging Jasmine, Aatish burst into tears. "I am sorry I lost you. Please forgive me. I will never let go of your hand."

The adoption centre called the police. They interrogated Mr Mishra.

He said, "My younger brother and sister in law, a childless couple, paid lots of money to a man in Agra to get this child, three years ago. The child received lots of love and was brought up as their own. She became part of our extended family and also received love from me and my younger sister. Unfortunately, my brother and sister in law died in a traffic accident."

"Why are you giving her up for adoption when she has become part of your family?" asked the officer.

Mr Mishra did not reply.

The police followed up the case. They discovered that Mr Mishra had applied to the court that in the absence of the will, he should be the beneficiary of his brother's large estate.

The police also interrogated his sister. She blurted out that there was a will made by her late brother which named their adopted child as the sole benefactor.

"Are you aware that Mr Mishra had applied to the court to transfer the whole estate to his name in the absence of the will?"

"Yes," replied the sister.

"Did you not object?" asked the police officer.

"Mr Mishra got me to sign a no objection certificate, promising to buy a flat for me in Delhi."

"Where is your late brother's will?" asked the officer.

"Mr Mishra destroyed it," she replied. "He told me that the will in favour of the child was invalid because the adoption was not registered, as the child was bought illegally from a gang."

After three weeks, the police agreed that Aatish and Tara could take Jasmine home. The officer said, "But you need to come back for court hearings."

"Why?"

"Mr Mishra has finally admitted to destroying the will and also gave us the details of the Agra man. We have arrested the man who sold your child. We seek to crush these evil child-abduction gangs."

The homecoming was joyous. The whole village celebrated Jasmine's return. They lit candles and oil lamps outside their houses. Sweets were distributed and there were fireworks.

Tara said cheerfully, "It feels like Diwali, the victory of good over evil."

Aatish's father told him, "The astrologer was right."

"What do you mean?" asked Aatish.

"Do you remember when I had a tattoo of Om and her name written on Jasmine's forearm and you were annoyed with me that Jasmine was too young to safely have a tattoo.?"

"Yes."

"Well, the astrologer had told me that year was not auspicious for the family. So, I made your plans to visit Kumbh mela in India to pray for the family. I'm sorry, son, how did I know that my granddaughter will be lost there? But Jasmine, my lovely gift from God, has been gifted back to us."

After hearing the story, Ranjit said, "Thank God Jasmine came back. What a traumatic journey for you all. I understand your feelings about not sending her abroad. But can I ask you what happened to the estate of Jasmine's adopted father?"

"I don't know. We never went back to India. We had our daughter back, why prolong our suffering?" replied Aatish.

40

That evening, Ranjit shared the conversations he had had with Aatish. "He doesn't want his daughter to leave Nepal."

"So I will stay in Nepal."

"They'll become suspicious. Why wouldn't a British university student return?"

Ranjit begged him to think with his brain and not be swayed by his emotions.

The next day, Jasmine wasn't in school.

A school day trip had been arranged to Kathmandu durbar square.

Reaching Kathmandu, Paul surveyed the free-for-all with cars, taxis, bicycles and vendors swerving past sleeping cows. With no signals and no traffic lights on the roads, he followed the other teacher and children when crossing the roads.

Paul watched a monkey reach into the bag of a tourist, who was busy looking at his mobile phone.

Arriving at Kathmandu durbar square, a UNESCO world heritage site, the teacher explained to the children, "This is a historically and culturally significant site for Nepal. This was the royal palace of our kings. It was first constructed in 3rd century. But major structures were added in later periods. The outer complex consists of a number of 16th-century temples built during the reign of Malla kings."

After the tour, there was an hour before the bus returned to their village.

The children opened their lunch boxes and sat down.

Paul had seen some travel agencies outside the durbar. There was a small shop advertising, "the best trekking trips at very reasonable prices."

Paul asked the agent, "Do you do Everest base helicopter flights?"

"We can arrange anything at very reasonable prices."

"What would be the cost of Everest base helicopter flight?"

"The charge is two thousand American dollars for one person but I will offer this to you for only one thousand American dollars for one person."

"No, too much. I am interested in buying for two people."

"How much can you pay today in cash?" asked the agent.

"One thousand American dollars for two people."

"Sure, if you pay now in cash," replied the agent.

Paul was pleased that he had US dollars in cash to pay. *What a bargain.*

Quickly taking the cash, the agent gave Paul a piece of paper. "This is the receipt for two people and the details of flights from Kathmandu."

"I want the helicopter flight with no fixed date so I can decide which day to go," said Paul.

"Sure, you can take the flight any day," promised the agent.

Paul left overjoyed at his surprise gift for Jasmine. He knew how much she'd enjoy sharing the panoramic views of the majestic Himalayas with him.

The next day, Paul telephoned the number on the receipt.

"I have an Everest base helicopter flight booked with you. Which days are available?"

"I'm sorry, we only do Himalayan rescue flights. We are a service for medical evacuations of trekkers who require urgent medical attention and care," replied the lady.

"But the travel agent gave me a receipt for your flight," insisted Paul.

"It is a mistake. Travel agents are not allowed to sell our flights. You'd better complain to the travel agent." She put the phone down.

Worried, Paul took a bus to Kathmandu.

Outside durbar square, the small shop was closed. The travel agency board had disappeared. Paul asked the neighbouring shop, "There was a travel shop next to you?"

"People use this corner and then disappear. It is all very suspicious."

"How do I contact that travel agent?" asked Paul.

The man shrugged his shoulders.

Sitting in the bus going back, Paul thought, *What an idiot I am to have trusted that agent.*

Suffering the pain of being scammed out of so much money, he felt the pain he had inflicted on Pinky. Tears of shame welled up in his eyes.

41

Next day at school, Jasmine avoided Paul.

At the end of the school day, Paul finally managed to catch up with her. "Please tell me if I've done something wrong but don't avoid me. It hurts me."

With tears in her eyes, she replied, "It is not my intention to hurt you. I'm confused. I cannot go against the wishes of my father so I will never emigrate."

"That's why I have decided to spend my life with you in Nepal."

"Are you sure?"

"Completely."

She hugged him, for a moment forgetting they were still in school. She looked around nervously.

They left the school and planned to meet secretly until both their families agreed to their marriage.

One day, sitting together at a waterfall in the forest, they heard three short bursts of noise.

In a moment, policemen with guns surrounded them.

Shouting in Nepali language, they started kicking Paul. He was pushed to the ground.

One policeman shouted, "Hang him with this rope." They put a rope around his neck.

"Leave him alone. He is British. Leave him please," pleaded Jasmine.

With a racing mind and pounding heart, Paul felt horrified, disorientated and dumbstruck.

"Where am I? Why am I bleeding?" Paul's mind went blank.

Suddenly, all the policemen were running up the hill, leaving Paul on the ground with a rope around his neck.

Jasmine removed the rope and helped him up.

Paul was badly bruised and battered. "What happened?" he asked.

"Police suspected you of being a maoist," replied Jasmine. "They are communists fighting the government and monarchy to achieve what they call a just and equal society. It is an armed struggle. They have killed policemen."

"I thought the police would kill me," whispered Paul.

"You were lucky. I heard a message on their walkie talkies that the maoist gunman was on the hill, so they ran up the hill. I'm sorry you suffered so much."

Paul made her promise that she would not tell anyone about the encounter.

"I won't even tell my father," said Paul. "I'll say I fell."

Reaching Paul's house, Jasmine took him in.

His dad was worried. "What happened?"

"He slipped and fell down," replied Jasmine. "Please make sure he sees a doctor tomorrow."

Paul slowly recovered. Jasmine visited every day.

One day she said, "I am glad to see you are recovering well."

"But my mental trauma is not getting better. I can't sleep for flashbacks of rope and hanging."

Jasmine held his hands tightly. "I'll help you to get better."

Jasmine took him to a festival in the neighbouring town. Vibrant with colourful stalls, it was full of families with children running between food and ice cream stalls. The funfair was like in UK with lots of children's rides and a mini version of the ferris wheel, only the wheels were pushed manually by men.

Paul was attracted to a crowd around the snake charmer.

In his colourful clothes and headgear, the snake charmer was swaying his long flute side to side while playing music. Paul noticed that the cobra, a very poisonous snake, was intermittently striking the flute. *That's why the flute is long*, he thought.

The snake charmer opened three other bamboo baskets and another snake rose up from each basket. Now, four black cobras hissing with raised hoods were swaying around the long flute.

"What an amazing scene," murmured Paul.

At the end, the snake charmer pushed each snake into the basket and covered it with the cloth.

Paul gave some money to the charmer.

Intrigued, Paul asked in Hindi, "Don't the snakes bite you?"

"Yes, but we remove their fangs."

"That's cruel," Paul retorted.

"But their fangs grow back," replied the snake charmer. "It is our livelihood."

"Where do you get these snakes from?" asked Paul.

"We catch them in forests and from riverbanks. During summer, they hide in shady, cool areas because the bubbling poison inside is like lava from a volcano, burning hot and bloodthirsty. People don't give us much money. I have to feed my family and the snakes. Sometimes, people call us to remove snakes from their homes but we are only paid if we catch the snakes."

Jasmine told Paul that some people believe snakes are sacred and regularly offer them milk to drink.

"Why don't you sell the poison from snakes for antivenom treatment of snake bites?"

"Only some snake charmers are recruited," he replied.

Paul wished him well and as they walked away, Jasmine remarked what a learning experience they'd had.

Paul replied, "Yes, but snakes find shady areas on hot days because they are cold-blooded."

Next, they joined a crowd watching a street entertainer performing a bear dance.

"I didn't know bears could dance," said Paul. "To me, you don't go near bears, they can kill, and here the man is ordering a bear to dance!"

The bear did flips, stood on its two feet and obeyed all the orders while people clapped.

"Training a powerful majestic bear to dance on the orders of a man must involve cruelty. It doesn't seem fair," insisted Paul.

Jasmine agreed. "It is a cruel process. They catch baby bears. Separated from the mother bear, they are isolated and put in cages."

"I hope this practice is banned," said Paul.

Next, they saw a puppet show in Nepali language.

"They are telling a tale of love," explained Jasmine.

The next big crowd was at a performance of three monkeys with running commentary in Nepali language.

"One is a female monkey. The two male monkeys are trying hard to woo her but she puts on airs and acts indifferent and difficult," translated Jasmine.

The last show they saw was a young girl walking the tightrope while balancing pots on her head. The tightrope was about ten feet above the ground. She had five traditional pots of different sizes over each other so on her head was the biggest size and on the top was the smallest pot. In her hands, she was holding a long stick to help her to balance.

Watching her bouncing on the rope, Paul found himself holding his breath.

He pointed, "Look at that anxious man watching her from below the rope."

"Maybe he is her father watching her so that if she loses balance, he will catch her. Many of these young girls are earning for their family."

The next act made Paul dizzy. She was riding a wheel on the rope. "What a risk this young girl takes to earn some money."

On completion of this act, there was a thunderous applause.

Jasmine said, "This girl is very talented."

But Paul was worried for her. "She must be around ten years old. She walks on a rope tied between two poles, about thirty feet of rope, which is about ten feet above the ground. Repeating this act many times a day without any protective gear is dangerous. If she trips and falls, her bones will be fractured and I shudder to think what will happen if she falls on her head. She does not even wear a helmet. Children should never be allowed to take such risks."

Jasmine said that family circumstances make children work but she agreed that the risks were too many.

After eating at the food stalls, they left the fair happy.

"Thank you, Jasmine. It was a thoroughly entertaining day," said Paul.

42

Paul had daily arguments with his dad, "I beg you to visit Jasmine's house and tell Aatish you agree to me staying in Nepal after our marriage."

"But I don't agree that your marriage is only allowed if you spend all your life in Nepal. Anyway, who is he to decide how my son spends his life?"

"He is Jasmine's father. In Nepal, fathers decide the daughter's marriage, don't you get it?"

"No, I don't get it."

"You are selfish and jealous." Paul angrily banged the door and left. Jasmine had invited him to a friend's house to celebrate her son's birth.

Outside the house was a noisy group of women, but they looked masculine. Wearing glittering jewellery and shining saris with heavy makeup on their faces, they were singing loudly and dancing.

"Who are they?" asked Paul.

"They are Hijras," replied Jasmine, and she narrated a story of a friend's brother, Abdul.

It was a prolonged labour. The village midwife was relieved when Mumtaz delivered.

Wiping sweat from her brow, in the stifling summer heat, Mumtaz asked her midwife, "Is it a boy or a girl?"

The midwife replied, "I don't know."

Mumtaz said, "I am not in a state to joke around. Please answer my question."

The midwife replied, "Well, he has a very small penis but also a small vaginal opening and ..."

Mumtaz exclaimed, "Thank God it's a boy. I already have four daughters. My husband Shabir threatened me that if I don't give him a son this time, he will marry again." She hugged the baby.

Shabir, a car mechanic, was over the moon. Distributing sweets in celebration, he told his neighbours, "Now I have a son to carry my family name. His name will be Abdul."

Shabir's mother told Mumtaz, "I never thought you were capable of giving me a grandson. I was already looking for a girl to marry my son again. You should thank God."

Mumtaz hated her mother-in-law for interfering but was frightened as Shabir always listened to his mother. She dare not offend her. Bowing and touching her feet, she said, "It is only because of your blessings."

The old woman was pleased. She put a black mark on the baby's cheek and said, "This is to prevent any evil eye cast on my grandson."

Outside the house, there was loud singing and dancing. The dancers wore glittering saris, faces heavily coated with makeup.

Shabir gave them money but they wanted more.

"Give them what they ask for. They have the power to turn their blessings into curses," said Shabir's mother.

Mumtaz knew that these people were called Hijras – the intersex people.

They gatecrashed weddings and visited houses with newborns and demanded money for giving their blessings. They danced, singing bawdy songs, and left with fistfuls of rupees.

Mumtaz thought, They'll recognise wedding houses by the colourful lights hanging on them, but how do they come to know which houses have newborn babies? Is their intelligence network so good? They live in their own communities but check newborn babies and if they suspect the baby is intersex, is it taken away?

Mumtaz felt frightened. She held the baby tightly and decided to keep her child away from the Hijra community.

One day, Shabir's mother wanted to give the baby a bath. She started undressing Abdul. Mumtaz's heart pounded with fear. The doorbell rang. It was her mother-in-law's friend. Mumtaz quickly covered Abdul. She heaved a sigh of relief.

As Abdul grew up, he played with dolls. He once made his sisters dress him in girls' clothes and put makeup and lipstick on him.

That day, Shabir walked in and flew into a rage.

He shouted, "What the hell is this? You sisters must keep away from him. You are a bad influence. He is a boy, he shouldn't copy you."

At five years old, Abdul started primary school. He was frightened of using the boys' toilet. Some boys taunted him. "You are a sissy." He was bullied daily.

He cried and pleaded with his mother. "I don't want to go to school. They call me names. They say, you look like a girl, your gestures are also girlish. No-one wants to be my friend."

It was heartrending. Every time she took Abdul to school, he would refuse to leave her side. She saw the fear in his eyes. She would leave him with a teacher and run, his cries ringing in her ears.

One day, a stone landed in their sitting room. The window shattered. Shabir ran outside, caught the boy and beat him up.

A neighbour asked Shabir, "How many will you beat up? Everyone is talking. They don't want a Hijra living in our community."

Shabir came home furious. He picked up Abdul and left the house.

Mumtaz did not sleep all night. Early morning, there was a knock on the door. She quickly opened it. Shabir was alone.

She asked, "Where is Abdul?"

"He is with his family," he replied.

"What you mean?" she asked anxiously.

"He is safe with his Hijra community."

She sobbed and pleaded with him. "He is our child. Have fear of God. Please bring him back."

Shabir pushed her away.

The sisters stopped eating, grief-stricken. They loved Abdul.

Mumtaz wanted to feed them but they refused. The eldest sister said, "We should be punished. We are the bad influence."

Mumtaz hugged them. She told them, "No, you are not responsible. God made him different because he loved him. I'll get him back."

She made enquiries and managed to trace the community Shabir had visited with Abdul. Shocked to find that this Hijra community were working as sex workers, she had to pay money to see Abdul. He was being kept in a small windowless room. There was an untouched plate of food. A tall muscular woman wearing a sari with heavy facial makeup was guarding the room.

She looked at Mumtaz and said, "You are a petite woman with indomitable spirit. You are very brave to come here."

Mumtaz said, "I and my daughters love Abdul. He may be Hijra but he is a God's gift to us. He belongs to my family. You can take my life but I will take him home."

The Hijra said, "People are frightened of us. They think that we are not good people. You have called us God's gift. It is my duty to help you."

She opened the back door. Mumtaz fled with Abdul.

At home, the sisters were ecstatic. Love and laughter had returned to their home.

When Shabir came home that evening, his face turned red with anger. He locked himself in his bedroom and refused to come out. Next day, Shabir left the house early. The news spread in the neighbourhood. The men started peeping into their house. They would whistle on seeing Abdul.

Mumtaz would not let Abdul leave the house. At night, she slept with her hands around him.

Next morning when she woke up, Abdul was not in the room. She searched the house in vain. Then she saw Shabir walk into the house, staggering like a drunk.

"Please, God, forgive me."

"Why, what have you done?"

He was shaking and sweating. He whispered, "It was a matter of family honour."

She saw the blood on his shirt and fainted.

"What a sad ending. How brave your friend's mother was. How is she now?" asked Paul.

"She left her husband and moved with her daughters to Kathmandu where she fights for the rights of Hijra people in Nepal," replied Jasmine.

"She is truly inspirational," said Paul.

Jasmine agreed. "Mumtaz is remarkable in what she has achieved for the Hijra in improving their lives."

Walking back to her village, Jasmine told Paul, "My parents would like to invite you and your dad to dinner. Will you come?"

43

Remembering her loneliness and hopelessness after she was falsely diagnosed with dementia, Pinky decided to apply as a volunteer for a dementia charity in Bradford.

In the training class, she asked, "I dance well to Bollywood Indian music. Can I use my dance and music to entertain people with dementia?"

"Sure, but use music which is soothing," was the reply.

Pinky joined a group of volunteers who visited care homes housing dementia residents.

Her dance to the 90s soft Bollywood music was a success. A lady who sat on her chair all day without talking or connection with her loved ones, got up and joined Pinky when the music started. Others clapped with the music.

The care home staff were surprised. One exclaimed, "The power of music."

On one of these visits, a woman was screaming, "Blood, blood..."

Pinky asked in Punjabi, "Blood where?"

She pointed to the windows. Pinky looked inside and outside the windows but there was no blood.

Her carer told Pinky that since onset of dementia, she repeatedly spoke of seeing blood.

"She has forgotten most of her memories but retained this memory of partition in India, when she saw so much bloodshed on both sides of the newly created border between India and Pakistan. This was in 1947, when after three hundred years in India, the British finally left.

"The other memory she has retained is a celebration of harvesting season in Punjab. She and her teenage friends would tie colourful swings to the trees.

"They sang traditional songs and would swing higher and higher. It was spring and the fields had blossomed with mustard flowers, a carpet of yellow flowers all around. When her daughter puts on the traditional harvest song, she will say with a smile on her face, *swing swing push push...*"

Pinky wondered if the most traumatic and intensely happy memories are lost much later than other memories in dementia.

One sunny day, Pinky and other volunteers took some residents to the woodlands. Holding hands, they walked slowly.

The birds were singing. One of the residents stopped with his mouth slightly open and head tilted forward as if trying to hear or see the bird. The volunteer pointed at the tree. As he looked up, the bird flew out. He clapped. Pinky joined in the clapping, happy to see a smile on the man's face.

They sat down in the open green space next to the winding river.

The volunteers served sandwiches, crisps and drinks.

Seeing the calmness on the faces of dementia patients was a satisfying experience for Pinky. It was as if immersing themselves in nature was the tonic they needed. One of them was Ian.

Suddenly, he started to swear, scream and shout at some noisy children throwing stones in the river. His eyes widened in fear. Pinky held his hands and whispered, "Ian, you are safe. Don't worry…"

Ian calmed down.

A minibus trip to Llandudno, North Wales, was organised for dementia sufferers and their carers. These are the carers who look after family members in their own homes.

In her training, Pinky had been taught that carers need breaks to give relief from twenty-four-hour care and compassion.

The drive from Bradford took more than two hours. Llandudno is a Victorian seaside resort with a long pier stretched out into the Irish Sea. It is lined with shops, cafes, bars and food stalls. Children were enjoying the funfair rides.

When they reached the end of the pier, they saw on either side of Llandudno Bay arising from the sea, two headlands called Great Orme and Little Orme.

Suddenly a mist appeared at the bottom of Little Orme as if it too was arising from the sea. Soon, the whole of the headland was covered with mist. Pinky thought it looked like an Indian bride with a greyish veil, magical and mystical.

Stopping at the food stalls, they ordered fish, chips, burgers, hotdogs and a double cheeseburger.

Pinky led one Alzheimer's sufferer, James, to a bench on the seafront.

As James started eating, a seagull swooped down, snatched the fish and some chips from his hands and flew away. "Thief!" screamed James, waving his arms around as more seagulls circled overhead.

Seeing his fast breathing and shaking hands, Pinky took

TSUNAMI OF GREED

James back to the fish and chip shop. This time they entered a covered seating area. There they met a carer who said, "No safety here also." She told Pinky that while eating her chicken sandwich, she'd felt a sudden heavy weight on her back. It was a big seagull on her shoulder, which took a swing at her table, snatching the sandwich and knocking off her chips and drink.

After eating, they walked to their minibus. Pinky felt a plop on her head followed by wetness, loads of wetness. Everyone was laughing hysterically. Someone told her, "You got a seagull poo on your head. It'll bring you luck."

Pinky saw a hotel and was relieved to clean up her hair in its facilities.

Back in the minibus, they headed onto the coastal road, which offered spectacular views of the sea and the massive cliffs. Stopping at the cliff with stunning sea views, they got down and took lots of photographs. The carers were relaxed as they could take off their carer's hat and savour the feeling of having a break, enjoying the view of sheer cliffs and the sea. Goats, lambs and sheep roamed free along the grass banks.

Pinky had read that these goats in Great Orme originated from India. According to local people, they are good weather forecasters, making their way to the lower, more sheltered southern slopes when rain is on its way. Maybe one day, they'd be TV weather presenters!

One person with dementia started walking towards a little lamb. Suddenly, a sheep jumped up and led the baby away from his path. Pinky thought, *Sheep are so protective of their young just like human mothers.*

On the way again, a side road led them to the summit of Great Orme.

At the summit, they got down from the minibus. Next to the carpark in the field, were more sheep. The cute lambs were running fast behind their mothers as if not to be left behind.

While taking a photograph of a carer called Lynn with her mother, Pinky managed to catch a little lamb jumping in the air. When Lynn saw the photograph, she said, "I was a perfectionist at work but had to leave my job to look after my mother when she was diagnosed with dementia. Now, I aim not for perfection but for moments of pleasure like this photograph with my mother. Thank you, Pinky."

Pinky felt so much respect for carers of family members.

It was time for tea and cakes.

Coming out of the cafeteria, they sat down on the grass on top of the hill.

Looking down, there was a pretty little church with a large cemetery, a lighthouse and sea in the background.

Richard, a volunteer who had visited the church in the past said, "It is a 12th-century church. Amidst the hill, it offers serenity and spectacular views of the sea. The lighthouse was erected in 1862 but is not in use now."

One of dementia patients whispered, "Light is land." He was an ex sailor.

On the summit is the Great Orme visitor centre.

There was a photograph of the Great Orme summit shrouded in cloud and sea mist.

Pinky thought, *We were lucky. We had good weather with no mist and good clear views.*

She liked a poem by John Ruskin, Victorian artist and writer, displayed in the centre.

> *Serenely calm and quiet days. Sunshine and blue skies.*
> *Hot sunshine, baking the rocks.*
>
> *Light reflecting from white rocks giving the Great*
> *Orme an extra special glow. There is really no such*

thing as bad weather, only different kinds of good weather.

Walking back to the carpark, they saw a station for Great Orme Tramway.

Richard explained, "The cable-hauled tramway is over one hundred years old and still popular with tourists visiting Llandudno."

On driving back, they saw a sign.

Great Orme Bronze Age Mines.

Richard explained this was "the world's largest prehistoric copper mine, over three thousand and five hundred years old."

Pinky asked, "Do you come to Llandudno often?"

Richard nodded. "I love Wales. On my last visit, I went on the Snowdonia Mountain Railway up to the summit. It's the highest mountain in Wales and England. On the summit of Mount Snowdonia, I felt on top of the world. Next time I'll walk. It'll take four hours climbing up and coming down. I can enjoy the waterfalls and views on the trek."

On the way back to Bradford, all agreed the trip was a roaring success. Despite her initial nerves, Pinky offered to volunteer for any more day trips.

44

Paul was awoken by a loud bang.

The ceiling fan was moving. Why would anyone switch the fan on in this cold night? The pictures had fallen off the wall.

Suddenly, the ground began shaking violently.

Paul jumped out of the bed, shouting, "Dad, get out. It's an earthquake."

As they rushed out into the open, the ceiling crashed and a blast of dust and rubble followed them out of the front door.

Outside, the surface of the path was rolling. Ground waves up to a metre high moved like giant ripples.

Paul thought, *I am on land, why I am seeing sea waves?*

Suddenly, the ground shaking stopped and the waves disappeared. The earthquake could not have lasted more than a minute but it felt like hours.

Paul started running to Jasmine's village.

Seeing houses crumbled to dust, some buried in the ground and others on the hillside gone, Paul's heart thundered. He raced even faster, avoiding the ground cracks in his path.

Reaching Jasmine's house, he watched with numb horror and disbelief. He went cold at the thought of Jasmine buried under the rubble. Her house had collapsed. The brick walls would have crumbled. Paul frantically started pulling away bricks, timber and other rubble.

Realising the challenge, he shouted for help. People were moving around in a dazed state. He talked to them and explained that they could help by working together to save lives. They started digging through the rubble with their bare hands. After few hours, exhausted from the work, they wanted rest.

Paul asked, "Is there anyone with tools for digging?"

One farmer brought pickaxes he used for digging the soil.

Another farmer brought more tools.

While Paul was digging, he shouted at others, "All quiet, can you hear?"

Yes, a voice was heard from the rubble.

Paul shouted loudly, "Don't worry, we are going to get you out safely."

They all started working harder and more carefully.

The cries for help were getting louder.

Dust covered and exhausted from digging, Paul finally pulled her out alive. He hugged Jasmine and covered her with his jacket.

Jasmine was crying, "Where are my mum and dad?"

"We will carry on digging until we find your parents," promised Paul.

But at nightfall, they had to rest.

Paul couldn't sleep. Each time he closed his eyes, he heard children crying for help, but he was not able to reach them. As daylight appeared, he woke the other helpers. They were all sleeping in the open, shivering through the cold mountain night.

The sirens were heard. It was a relief to see ambulances and fire-brigade vehicles approaching. There were specialists from different countries who help in earthquake rescues. Special machinery had arrived. The medical team were there also.

"These are specially trained dogs from England. These dogs can smell humans buried alive. When they locate a survivor, they bark to alert us," said the professional rescuer from Liverpool. He told Paul his rescue dog had saved many lives all around the world.

Paul awoke Jasmine and told her, "Help has come from Kathmandu with specialists and machinery. Soon, your mum and dad will be safely taken out."

"How's your dad?" asked Jasmine.

"He must be fine. We got out from our house in the nick of time. It was a narrow escape."

"You should check on him," she advised.

Paul went to his house but the house was rubble. Going around the school building, he was surprised that except for some cracks, the building had survived the earthquake.

He went in and found Ranjit sleeping on the bench in the school corridor. Paul went into the kitchen and found food. He filled boxes with supplies. In the store room, he found blankets. With Ranjit's help, he got the boxes and warm blankets to the village people sleeping outdoors.

The rescue teams started work as soon as they arrived.

After a few hours, there was a loud cheer. A child had been brought out alive. Next rescued was an older woman. She was rushed to the ambulance.

Journalists were taking photographs.

Now, the rescuers were at Jasmine's house, digging and listening.

It was midday and getting hotter. They decided to take a break.

But the rescue dog started barking. He was running around in circles at one place.

The rescuers placed the listening devices that magnify sounds and fitted cameras that can see through cracks in the rubble at the site indicated by the dog.

It seemed the cameras detected something. The team were now digging carefully while looking at the cameras.

Paul was praying, "Please God, save Jasmine's mum and dad."

The rescuers had now stopped. They were listening through the cracks in the rubble.

The senior rescuer discussed with the fire fighters. They used a stick to pass a bottle of water through the crack. It seemed the crack opening was made wider until a fire fighter was lowered tied to a rope.

Paul's heart pounded against his chest. It seemed ages but then he saw someone hauled up. It was Jasmine's mother. She was put on a stretcher and rushed to the waiting ambulance.

Paul ran to Jasmine to give her the good news.

Despite her sprained and bruised legs, Jasmine wanted to be at the rescue site. With support from Paul, she managed to reach her house.

The villagers were clapping. Then Jasmine saw her father lifted out from the rubble. She burst into tears of joy.

Whilst journalists were taking his photograph, the first question Aatish asked was, "Is my daughter Jasmine safe?"

"Yes, yes, Jasmine is safe," shouted Paul.

"Tell us what happened to you?" asked a journalist.

"The walls collapsed, trapping me and my wife in a pile of rubble. I could move my arm and legs a little bit. I could breathe. I slept only to awake up and wonder if I was dead. I heard voices but didn't know if they were real. I was so thirsty that I drank my own urine. Thank you God and thanks to my rescuers."

Paul picked Jasmine up and took her to the ambulance, where her mother was being attended to by the medical team. When her father was brought to the ambulance, Jasmine could hardly believe her family was together again. Hugging her dad, she said, "I was so worried about both of you. It's a miracle."

She described how Paul had saved her.

Aatish hugged Paul. "Thank you, Paul. The ambulance is leaving for Kathmandu with me and my wife. Please look after Jasmine."

"I surely will," replied Paul.

Jasmine told Paul, "In Nepal, women fast on certain days for the long life of their husbands. In my mind, I am married to you so I will also fast for your long life."

"We will marry soon but we are already one soul, two bodies," replied Paul.

The rescuers were now working at other collapsed and buried village houses.

Paul helped Jasmine to slowly walk back to the school.

In the kitchen, he made a warm drink. Giving it to Jasmine, he said, "This is to celebrate the safe rescue of your parents."

Then with Ranjit, he packed food and water bottles and took them to the villagers.

Handing drinks to the rescuers he said, "You are my heroes. I salute your professionalism and determination."

When Paul gave a cup of hot tea and food to the dog handler from England, he said, "I love chai. I love food from the Indian subcontinent."

Paul petted the dog and fed him biscuits.

It was getting dark. Back at school premises, Paul helped Jasmine to a bench in the outer school corridor and covered her with a warm blanket.

He and Ranjit slept in the teachers' meeting room.

Paul awoke in the middle of night. A low rumble filled the air. The ground was shaking and the walls began to crumble and fall apart. When the shaking finally stopped, the air was filled with dust and smoke. He realised it was a violent aftershock and he was trapped in a heap of rubble.

He looked sideways to where his father was sleeping. It was pitch dark. He couldn't see a thing.

"Dad, are you alright?"

No reply came.

He wanted to check on his dad but something very heavy was crushing his leg. He was stuck there.

He cried for help again and again but no one came.

I hope Jasmine is safe, he thought.

All night, with his trapped leg, he was in severe pain.

Next morning, he heard voices and a dog barking.

"My heroes have come to save me and Dad."

He shouted again and again, "I am here. I am here. Help me."

After what seemed a long time, a light shone into the room.

"Don't worry, we are coming to help you," shouted a rescuer.

In the light, Paul looked sideways. His father was lying motionless in a big pool of blood. Tears filled Paul's eyes. *Has God punished us for what we did to Pinky?* Finally seeing the rescuers, he burst into tears.

They gave him some water. Paul pointed at his dad. "Can you help him?"

"Sorry, he's dead. His skull has been cracked open. He must have died instantly."

After clearing away the debris, they approached Paul's trapped right leg.

"Sorry, the leg is pinned down by very heavy concrete beams."

The medical team was called. The doctor told Paul that to save his life, he would have to amputate his right leg. "It was completely crushed under the weight of the debris. The firefighters can't release the leg from the fallen debris of the collapsed walls. I have decided to amputate the right leg below your knee. It will release you from the debris and save your life. Can I proceed now?"

In severe pain, Paul nodded.

The doctor gave an injection of morphine and tied a tourniquet. With the help of the rescuers, he carried out the procedure.

Paul was whisked out of the rubble.

He looked at his father with tears in his eyes. He folded his hands in prayer. "I wish I could have given Dad a respectable cremation."

The ambulance journey to Kathmandu was long and difficult. The roads were frequently blocked due to landslides. But many roads had deep cracks. Paul suffered excruciating pain and needed regular morphine.

At last, they reached the hospital. It was a scene of confusion and heartbreak. People were screaming, some with severe injuries, broken limbs and bleeding. Some had died. Others were awaiting attention.

In the overcrowded ward, Paul got a bed. He looked around. There was a sea of suffering. Patients on the floor cried out with pain.

He thought, *Oh God, why so much pain and suffering.* Tears gathered at the corner of his eyes.

All night, he could not sleep.

Early morning, he started shivering and feeling cold. The

nurse checked his temperature. His blood pressure was low. Feeling his cold clammy skin, she called the doctor.

Due to the massive influx of patients, medical students were drafted in. Attending Paul was a 4th-year medical student. He checked Paul and noted fever, increased heart rate and rapid breathing. He checked the wound from the amputation. After checking blood tests and urine for infection, he set up intravenous fluids and told the nurse to start antibiotics.

The consultant took the ward round with the medical student. Examining Paul, he found him confused and drowsy. Checking blood tests, he found that kidney and liver function tests were abnormal.

He told the medical student, "Do blood cultures immediately. They will tell us the type of infection, what antibiotic to give and sensitivities of different antibiotics."

He changed antibiotics from oral route to intravenous.

"Keep an eye on him," he told the medical student.

After three days, Paul developed difficulty breathing. His nurse had trouble rousing him. She called the medical student. He checked Paul's heart and lungs. The oxygen saturation was low. Oxygen was started. Liver and kidney function had deteriorated. The blood cultures showed the antibiotic being given was correct.

The medical student discussed with the consultant. "Despite the correct antibiotic being administered intravenously, Paul's condition is deteriorating. Why?"

"This is antimicrobial resistance. When bacteria develop the ability to defeat the drugs designed to kill them, the germs are not killed and continue to grow."

In the consultant's evening ward round he told Paul, "You have a serious infection which is not responding to normal antibiotics. The nurse tells me that you are from England. They have more advanced antibiotics, which can save your life. I would advise you to travel back. I have increased the dose of antibiotics. I will give you a letter detailing the treatment you have had."

The hospital contacted the British Embassy, who were planning evacuation of their injured citizens. Paul was put on the priority list.

That day, Jasmine found Paul. She had been searching in every hospital in Kathmandu. She was shocked to see how poor his condition was. He was drowsy. Holding his hands, tears welled up in her eyes. "I love you, Paul."

Paul opened his eyes.

The nurse told her that he would be going back to England soon.

She wrote a letter explaining that her mother was recovering in an another hospital and her father was looking after her.

She finished the letter, "I will wait for you all my life. After all, you are my soulmate, my husband." She wrote her address and contact telephone number. She put the letter in his pocket. She didn't want to leave his bedside but the nurse told her it was time to go.

When Jasmine returned next day, Paul had gone. She was devastated.

Paul was on the flight with other injured patients.

The British doctor was worried whether Paul would make the flight safely.

Reaching London, the waiting ambulance raced him to the hospital.

The doctors read the consultant's letter and immediately ordered investigations. With oxygen and intravenous newer antibiotics, Paul slowly recovered.

Reading Jasmine's letter, Paul realised how poorly he had

been. He wrote to Jasmine giving her the good news of his recovery.

Jasmine replied quickly, "I am so relieved to get your good news."

The junior doctor told him, "You are lucky. You could have had kidney failure and respiratory failure in Nepal. Your life was in danger."

With prosthetics and mobile aids, Paul could walk again. He was having regular physiotherapy.

One day, the police arrived and arrested him.

Paul wrote a long apology letter to Jasmine and explained why he was going to prison.

"I would have told you about my conviction when I met you in Nepal, but I didn't want to lose you. I am honest and God-fearing, a changed man now. I promise to be your good and caring husband."

He finished the letter, "In this country, sometimes you only spend half the term. So with a bit of luck, I may be free in three and half years. I plan to come back to you in Nepal after completing my sentence."

Jasmine replied, "I'll be waiting for you. I love you."

45

Paul's first day in prison started with a strip search. It was so humiliating, he felt his self-respect and dignity draining away.

Being locked in a cell like an animal in a cage was shocking. Sitting alone in the cell, Paul could see the door leading to the outside world but he was locked in his cell.

I never realised the value of freedom. But I deserve this. Didn't I take Pinky's freedom and dignity?

When he was permitted to leave his cell, Paul felt as if everyone was looking at him. It was an unnerving experience. He avoided eye contact and ironically was relieved to be back in his cell where he spent long periods locked inside.

One day in the prison grounds, there was a shout. "You freshie, go back to your country."

Paul looked up and saw a six feet, six inches tall muscular man approaching him. In a flash, Paul was on the ground. After pushing him, the man was raining kicks on him.

Prison officers came running and took him away. Shaken and bruised, Paul got up.

"He's a bully. Calls himself prison chief," said an officer, and asked if he needed to see the nurse. Paul declined.

Next day, he had a new cellmate. A six feet two inches, burly looking man with a glass eye and a long scar across his face.

Paul thought, *Now I am not safe inside or outside my cell.*

But appearances are deceptive. Kevin was kind to Paul. On being told about the kicking incident, he said, "If you don't stand up to people, you get pressured into doing things you don't want to do. I was in a good school. Because I was weak, the gangs used me to smuggle drugs. When I wanted to leave, I was threatened that my mother would be killed. I was frightened. Now, despite all the risks, I have no fear. "

Paul replied, "I don't have the guts to look them square in the eyes."

"Don't worry, I'll protect you," Kevin reassured Paul.

Paul told the story of his leg prosthesis and asked Kevin about his eye prosthesis, the glass eye.

"I came out of the pub one night, high as a kite. I felt something hit my right eye, there was excruciating pain. I could barely open my eye. I was seeing all black. My mate called the ambulance."

Kevin continued, "In the hospital, the doctor told me that I'd lost my right eye vision as I was shot in the right eye." He said, 'You have a hole in the right eye, the bullet went through your eye but did not pierce your brain.' After surgery, I was offered the glass eye. It is as good to me as a gang member. I take my eye out to frighten people!"

Paul thought, *what a brave and humorous man.*

Paul asked Kevin, "If you cry, do any tears come out of the right eye?"

"What a stupid question. My right eye is an empty eye socket, how can it cry!"

Paul taught Kevin chess and they spent hours playing together.

Jasmine's letters had stopped. In her last letter, she'd written, "I'm getting lots of pressure to marry. I refuse, but every week a new man with his family come to our house to see me. I'm truly sick and tired of my dad angrily shouting at me, 'You are purposely refusing the prospective grooms to insult me.' He can't understand that I love you and want to only marry you."

Paul was sick with worry. He'd seen many suicidal cases in the prison.

One day, Paul was surprised to see Pinky and Seema visiting him in the prison.

Paul touched their feet in respect. With tears flowing down his cheeks, he apologised profusely for the suffering Pinky had endured.

"I have already forgiven you," replied Pinky.

Paul told them about the death of his dad in the earthquake in Nepal and Pinky gave her condolences.

"After my release from prison, I'll come to Bradford for a few weeks to look after you."

"No, you keep away from Pinky," retorted Seema.

Time passed and one morning, the prison officer gave Paul the welcome news that he would be released early because of his good behaviour.

46

Having completed half of his sentence, Paul was released from prison.

He phoned Pinky to tell her that he was going back to Nepal to marry the girl he loved.

Pinky wished him a happy married life.

From London, he caught the flight to Nepal.

Arriving in Kathmandu, as the plane descended, Paul saw a mountain sticking up through the clouds. He thought of Jasmine's beautiful mountain village.

Sitting in the bus on way to the village, he remembered his ambulance journey after his amputation and losing his dad. Tears welled up in his eyes.

A man sat next to him. "You foreign, me speak English. A good volunteer job, me help you."

"Sorry, I don't want a volunteer job," said Paul.

The man abruptly left.

Paul noticed that he had moved to a seat next to another foreigner, maybe to continue with his *I speak English and me help*.

After Paul was cheated by the travel agent, he'd stopped trusting strangers like this one offering volunteer jobs.

On reaching the village, he walked with his luggage to Jasmine's house.

Aatish opened the door but did not look pleased to see Paul. Behind her dad was Jasmine. She hugged him tightly.

When Paul saw tears in her eyes, he asked, "Why are you crying?"

"These are tears of joy," she replied. "What a lovely surprise. Please come in."

Tara was also happy to see Paul. She quickly brought drinks and snacks.

Aatish asked Paul, "What are your plans in Nepal?"

"Sir, with your permission, I want to marry Jasmine. I promise to look after her."

"But you have no job, no house. How will you look after her?"

Jasmine replied, "Paul agreed to stay in Nepal after marriage because you demanded it. He has now returned for me and, Dad, if you refuse, I will never marry. I only want to marry Paul."

"What if he leaves you for England?" asked Aatish.

"After his jail sentence, he is a free man in UK but he still came back. Dad, please trust him."

Tara took Aatish to the next room. Jasmine held Paul's hand and whispered, "Don't worry, I will always stand with you."

Both parents returned.

Aatish said, "OK, I agree to the marriage. The date will be decided by the astrologer."

Jasmine jumped with joy and hugged her dad.

Aatish told Paul that until the marriage, he couldn't stay in their house as per Nepali custom. "But I will arrange for you to stay at our farm."

Next morning, Paul woke up late. Looking outside, there were the golden fields of rice. People were harvesting the rice by hand.

Buffaloes were roaming around. They provided fresh milk every day, some of which was converted to yoghurt. The farm worker was washing one of the buffalo.

Paul visited the school. The damaged building had been rebuilt.

The teachers were glad to see him. He also saw the headmaster, who told Paul, "At present, no teacher jobs are available but I will remember you for any vacancy."

Paul visited the room in the school where he lost his father. Feeling dizzy with a pounding heart, he quickly left.

Walking back through the village, he noticed some houses on the hill were still in a damaged state.

Next day, Paul got a message from the headmaster to see him.

When Paul visited his office, the headmaster explained that a teacher who was going to retire the following year had decided to leave early to look after her ailing mother-in-law.

"Would you like to start working in the school?"

"When do I start?"

"Tomorrow," replied the headmaster. "But there is no accommodation we can offer you."

Paul walked fast to Jasmine's house. Jasmine was thrilled. Aatish was pleased to hear the news and announced that he would buy a house in the village for them to live together after marriage.

Paul didn't like the idea of getting a dowry. This was prevalent in Nepal where a gift called a dowry was given by the bride's family to the groom.

He convinced Aatish that the house should only be in the name of his daughter, which he finally agreed.

Already at the house was the astrologer, who was studying their star signs.

"Your star signs match perfectly. Your marriage is made in heaven," said the astrologer. He gave the auspicious date for the marriage, which was only two weeks away.

Aatish took Tara, Jasmine and Paul to Kathmandu for a hectic day spent buying jewellery, bride and groom dress and gifts for the guests.

Next day, Paul and Jasmine went on a walk from their village.

The mountain speared the clouds above it. The clouds floating on the mountain rocks felt magical.

Paul was enchanted by the clouds, some sticking and clinging to the mountainside and some sitting on the cliff top as if resting after a long climb.

A string of low-hanging white clouds settled across the neck of the mountain like a warm wool scarf. But then one delicately turned into a silk scarf and hugged the shoulders of the mountain tops.

Walking up, Paul was tired and sat down.

"Are you OK?" asked Jasmine.

"With my prosthesis, I need to rest but we will walk further."

Sitting down with Paul, Jasmine asked, "Settling in Nepal after marriage, will you miss England?

"Yes, I will miss Pinky."

"Is this the lady your court case was ...?"

"Yes. She treated me like a son. She is my only relative there. Unfortunately, my dad was angry with Bobby, Pinky's husband. When he came to UK, he was employed by Bobby in his factory. They fought over money. My dad was sacked. After that, we struggled financially and my dad wanted revenge. When Bobby died, my father planned to take control of their estate. Sometimes I ask myself why I didn't stop him. Since I lost my mother in childhood, my relationship with my dad was one of respect and I never questioned him on any issue. Maybe I was frightened of him. But I am guilty because when my dad told me it was easy to cheat Pinky and become rich, greed overcame me."

They got up and continued hiking, surrounded by cloud.

Paul said, "It feels surreal."

But suddenly visibility was poor.

"It is like the fog in UK," said Paul.

They decided to walk back to their village. Paul looked back at the low floating clouds in the mountains. "Without you, I would have been a wandering lonely cloud," he said to Jasmine.

Jasmine hugged him. "We will float together in life."

As they walked down, the river in the distance was like a silver stream winding around the valley.

It was a lovely walk with magnificent views.

By the time they reached their village, the sun was painting the sky in varying shades of orange and red.

Time passed quickly but one night before the wedding was a ladies' celebration. Paul sneaked in with the help of Jasmine's friend.

The women were singing. Then they stood and formed a circle. A lady with a drum started playing with a stick on both sides. Moving around in a circle with hand movements on one side and then the other side in rhythmic manner to the beat of the drum, the dancers were in perfect synchronism.

"It is a treat to the eye," said Paul. "But what do you call this dance?" he asked.

"It is called Dhime Naach," replied the friend. "It is

performed during festivals and after the farmers reap a good harvest."

After the dance ended, the women sat down. There was a loud laughter and clapping.

"What are they laughing about?" asked Paul.

"One of the women was talking about her father-in-law in Nepali language," replied Jasmine's friend.

"Was it a joke? If so, can you tell me in English please."

"Her eighty-year-old father-in-law was calling his wife, 'My honey, my love, my darling'. A family member asked her father-in-law, 'I have noticed you have become romantic lately, calling your wife honey, darling.' He replied, 'Oh, not romantic. The last few months, I can't remember her name!'"

More laughter followed. Paul asked for more translation but the friend replied, "I cannot. These jokes are vulgar."

On the wedding day, Jasmine wore a red silk sari and heavy gold jewellery.

Paul wore a Nepali groom dress. It was a silk knee-length shirt, loose fitting trousers and a waistcoat. The shirt was cream coloured with red embroidery.

They exchanged the garland made of doobo, which is a certain type of grass that does not dry, indicating that the relationship will never break or dry.

Under a specially erected canopy, the Hindu priest recited sacred mantras as Paul and Jasmine walked around the sacred fire seven times with the knot tied between them.

The marriage ritual was completed when Paul put sindur (red vermilion powder) on Jasmine's head and tilhari (a holy necklace) around her neck.

The relatives and friends with gifts blessed the couple with tika, a crimson marking on the forehead. All wished them good luck in their life-long commitment. But one guest whispered to Paul, "It is a life-long imprisonment."

Next was the emotional scene where Aatish and Tara with tears in their eyes hugged Jasmine tightly. Jasmine burst into tears. Seeing Jasmine cry, tears welled up in Paul's eyes but he also remembered his dad and wished he was here.

Aatish also hugged Paul. "It is now your responsibility to look after my daughter."

Tara advised, "Jasmine, always wear sindur and pray for Paul's long life."

Sitting in the decorated car, the couple were on their way to their new house in the village to start their married life together.

ABOUT THE AUTHOR

My name is Surinder Singh Jolly and I am a retired medical doctor.

I was born and raised in Kenya and studied Medicine in India but moved to UK in 1979. In 2009, I was awarded an MBE by the Queen for services to medicine and healthcare.

After working in British national health service for three and a half decades, I retired in 2016. After retiring, I completed a course in creative writing and that started my journey to becoming an author.

My debut book, *Indian Whispers*, was published in 2021. This was also produced as an audiobook.

If you enjoy *Tsunami of Greed*, please help to spread the word by leaving a review on Amazon, Goodreads or any other suitable forum. These are a huge help to authors.

ALSO BY SURINDER SINGH JOLLY

Indian Whispers

www.ingramcontent.com/pod-product-compliance
Lightning Source LLC
LaVergne TN
LVHW041636060526
838200LV00040B/1589